Made by a Vampire

Las Vegas Vampires #5

SOPHIE SLADE

CONTENTS

PROLOGUE

Leila

Walking with our children—Jase, the equivalent of a twelve-year-old, and Sirena, the equivalent of a four-year-old—I can't help but notice how much they've grown. Dhampir children grow at an accelerated rate and will reach their full maturity at ten years of age. As I watched them, a part of me already missed their baby stages, but I want what all parents want… for my children to be happy, to grow up strong, to feel loved and protected.

And now, as a vampire, I can give them all those things.

In fact, it will take vampires to keep up with them. As dhampirs, they are half human and half vampire. As such, they have superhuman strength and need blood, but they don't crave it like vampires. Our friend Amy is a dhampir… super strong and intelligent, but the sunlight doesn't affect her the way it traditionally affects vampires, burning them to death. Nor does it affect my children.

After Lance and I first got together, I developed a sunlight serum that prevents the extreme radiation poisoning vampires receive from sunlight exposure, which causes them to spontaneously combust upon exposure.

When we met, my husband, Lance, was confined to the shadows, to a life of eternal darkness. But now, all that has changed.

Our children have also inherited my magical abilities. Unbeknownst to me, I'm from a long line of strong witches. But my powers didn't manifest completely until I turned. As a result, my dhampir children have my magical powers. I just wish this world would leave them in peace to grow up as normal children.

But they are far from normal… and so am I.

CHAPTER 1

Leila

"Where are we going, Mom?" Jase asked, fidgeting as he pulled at his tie.

I waited in the hallway, not wanting to ruin this for Amy, who had been working our "surprise" anniversary party for weeks. I pulled them to a stop and bent down to their level. "Aunt Amy planned a surprise for all of us, so we need to wait for Daddy."

Jase narrowed his eyes. "If it's a surprise, then why do you know about it?"

I smiled as I pushed a lock of his blond hair away from his lovely green eyes, a trait of both vampires and dhampirs.

"I'm good at guessing secrets."

With our superhuman hearing and sight, it would be nearly impossible for Amy to keep anything from Lance or me. We've known about this party for a while, but I told Lance that he needed to act surprised for Amy's sake.

Sirena laughed. "You can't keep secrets from vampires!"

I chuckled, nodding my head. Although it was true that we were vampires, the word sounded strange rolling off her tongue so easily. I guess I wanted to think of us as a typical human family, even though we were far from it.

I turned Sirena around and adjusted the bow on her frilly pink dress and brushed off her matching satin ballet slippers. "Yes, but we can't tell the humans what we are. You understand that. Don't you?"

Sirena scoffed as she skipped off. "Yes. Of course, Mommy!" She plopped down on the floor as her dark brown bob swayed just above her shoulders, turning her attention to her doll.

"And you understand, too. Don't you, Jase?" I asked as I

adjusted his tie.

He rolled his eyes. "Mom, I'm a little older than Sirena. Of course, I know!"

Although he looked many years older than his younger sister, technically, they were only one year apart. Within a few short years, they would look exactly the same age and will never age a day after that. I sighed at the thought.

"My, my!" Lance smiled as he walked into the hallway, taking my breath away as he always did. Even after the short time I'd known Lance, he still knocked me breathless with his dark brown hair, beautiful green eyes, and hard, muscled body that could stop traffic. "Don't you look handsome?" he asked Jase, placing his hand on his shoulder.

Jase lowered his eyes and blushed. "Dad!"

"Well, now, no matter how old you get, you'll still be my little boy." Lance sighed as he took Jase in, his smile fading.

"What's wrong?" I could always read Lance, especially now that I was a vampire. Hard telling how much he got away with and how many secrets he kept before that; I just didn't notice.

Lance shook his head slightly, barely noticeable. Then he leaned in conspiratorially. "I'll tell you later." Then he inhaled my scent and gently kissed my lips.

"Eww! Gross!" Jase scrunched up his nose, shaking his head.

Lance chuckled, arching an eyebrow as he took in our son. "When you get older and find the right girl, you won't think it's so gross anymore."

I burst out laughing.

Suddenly, Sirena jumped to her feet and skipped across the floor to Lance. Then she placed her hand on the side of her mouth and stage-whispered, "Are you ready to be surprised, Daddy?"

He laughed. "I guess so." He looked over at me and smiled, raising his eyebrows. "Ready?"

I shrugged. "As ready as I'll ever be." Then he lowered his voice. "You look divine, by the way."

"And you look very handsome." I smiled, giving Jase's shoulder a gentle squeeze, but he shrugged me off.

"Let's go already!" Jase scoffed. "Aunt Amy will be disappointed if we don't hurry up."

He was right. Inside, Amy was complaining to Drake Summerfield, wondering what was taking us so long. It's funny how much I'd missed before I became a vampire.

Lance chuckled. "Vampire hearing."

"Dhampir." Jase headed toward the door.

"No, sir." Lance stopped him. "We're going in as a family." Then he wrapped his arm around me, and we walked inside the main dining hall.

"Surprise!" everyone yelled at once, rising to their feet as they clapped loudly.

Walking in with everyone clapping for us brought back memories of when we were married just a year ago. A lot had happened during that time, but it already seemed to be a lifetime ago.

"Wow!" I said, feigning surprise.

"Everyone, thank you so much for coming!" Lance chuckled and then pulled Amy in for a hug. "You did a great job keeping it secret."

She burst out laughing and gave him a playful slap on the stomach. Then her eyes shot over to me. "You weren't supposed to tell him!"

I shrugged. "If I didn't tell him something, he would have been off galivanting to the hospital or something."

"Well, it's about time you got here!" Rosa laughed as she pulled me in for a hug. She smelled so good, but I'd learned how to control my thirst over the past few months. Besides, I wouldn't bite Rosa, anyway. "Wow! You look great! There's no way you look like you had two kids!" she chuckled, leaning in conspiratorially. "And you never will." Then she gave me a wink.

I laughed, releasing her. "Thanks, Rosa! I'm so glad you and Henry came!" I hugged her again. "I've missed you!"

She gave me an air kiss over my cheek and smiled when she pulled back. "I've missed you, too, girlie." Her lips curled into a smile as she gave Amy a sly look, nodding toward her. "This one here is a slave driver!"

"Oh, I'm the best boss you've ever had, and don't you forget it!" Amy teased.

"You're not my boss," Rosa said flatly.

"No, but I am!" Drake pulled her in for a hug, too.

"Well, that's a given," Rosa teased. Drake was the Hospital Administrator and my old boss. Then he pulled me in for a hug and shook Lance's hand. "Congratulations! May you both have a long and happy marriage!"

"Thanks, Drake," Lance beamed. "Thanks for coming."

He chuckled as he gave Lance a manly slap on the back. "I wouldn't have missed this for the world!"

"One of these days, we'll have to set you up with someone, and you can join me in the ranks of happily married men," Lance teased.

Drake scoffed. "Yeah. Keep dreaming." In all the time I'd known him, he'd dated, but I never saw him with anyone serious. But you never know when lightning will strike.

Drake not only worked at Southside Medical Hospital, he was also the head of the South Coven and had come to our aid more times than I cared to remember.

Amy smiled as she looked her arm in mine. "Well, follow me, and let's get this show on the road!" She headed toward the main table, and we followed. Jase was still fidgeting with his tie, so Amy took it off, laid it on the table, and unbuttoned the top two buttons of his dress shirt. "Better?"

A broad smile spread across his face as he nodded. "Thanks, Aunt Amy!"

I laughed, shaking my head. "He was supposed to leave it on, at least until after dinner."

Amy arched an eyebrow. "So, is Lance wearing a tie?"

I chuckled. "You have a point." Actually, he rarely wore ties, but he always looked dressed up and looked debonaire.

Lance laughed as he lifted our daughter into his arms and placed his hand on my back. "Leila and I would like to thank all of you for coming today and for your well wishes! Please, join us in celebrating our wedding anniversary!"

Everyone clapped as they took their seats. Then Chef Faustino, the head chef at the castle, stepped to the front of the room and folded his hands. "Tonight, for your dining pleasure and in honor of Mr. and Dr. Steel...." Everyone laughed. "I have prepared for you a traditional Medieval banquet! Enjoy!"

Everyone clapped and "ooed" and "ahhed" as Chef Faustino headed back to the kitchen. A moment later, servers handed out plates while other servers carried around platters and bowls filled with food.

A gentleman approached, carrying a platter of roast beef and a fork. "Would you care for some, Dr. Steel?"

I nodded. "Yes, please."

He served me two slices and then moved on to Lance. I cut up one of the slices for Sirena, laid it on her plate, and she started eating right away.

As a vampire, food still tasted good to me, but not as good as it did when I was human. But that was probably a good thing.

"Everything looks so good!" Lance gushed, letting the servers fill up his plate. Lance underwent two of the three treatments needed to become human when Xander stopped him so he could save me. But when his vampire came back fully, he came back with a vengeance. Lance was now a super vampire, if that even was such a thing.

"Are you having fun?" I whispered in Lance's ear.

He nodded, smiling as he arched an eyebrow, looking deeply into my eyes. "Are you?"

A smile lit my lips. "As long as I'm with you, I have fun."

"Umm...." He leaned in close and whispered, "I'll remind you of that later."

I laughed, shaking my head. "You'll never change."

"Nope!" Then he gave me a sexy smile. "But would you want me to?"

I shook my head. "Not on your life."

He took a sip of his wine. "So, you're glad I didn't turn human again?"

"I'll love you no matter what, human or vampire. It matters not to me."

He chuckled. "Now you're starting to sound like me."

I shrugged. "Well, I've been hanging out with you long enough."

"Lucky me." He kissed my nose and then went back to his meal.

I took a few more things for Sirena and myself, while Lance oversaw Jase. But every time Lance tried to help him with something, Jase brushed him off, telling him that he could do it.

But throughout the meal, I noticed that Lance seemed a bit off.

"What's wrong?" I took a sip of my wine, waiting.

Lance let out a deep breath, his smile fading as he dabbed at the corners of his mouth. "I'll tell you later."

"That's what you said when you came downstairs." I scooped some potatoes onto Sirena's plate, and she dug in immediately. "Tell me now."

He glanced down at our little girl and shook his head. "Soon."

I arched an eyebrow. "Promise?"

He nodded, a smile coloring his lips. "Yes, of course."

I took another sip of my wine and continued eating. Since I'd met Lance, he had always been protective. And now that I was a vampire, he still was. I made a mental note to talk to him about it later. As a vampire, I didn't need as much protection. But it was in his nature... who he was. And like I'd told him, I wouldn't want him to change in the slightest.

After the meal was finished and dessert was served, the string quartet began to play, and people started milling about on the dancefloor, swaying to the music.

"Would you like to dance?" Lance smiled as he looked into my eyes.

"I thought you'd never ask." I stood, and Sirena held her hands up to Lance.

"Come here, baby girl." He took her, and she laid her head on his shoulder as he rose to his feet.

"Lance, she's sleepy." I shrugged. "We can dance later."

One corner of his lips curled into a sly smile. "No, I have other plans for you later."

"Oh? You do, huh?" I stood and let him take my hand.

"Count on it." But before we left the table, a crease formed between his eyes, and his expression turned serious. "Amy, could you keep an eye on Jase for us, please?"

Amy nodded, her smile fading, too. "Don't worry. He's safe with me."

"Oh, come on!" Jase huffed. "I don't need a babysitter!"

"Oh, no?" Addie approached the table, smiling. "Then how about a dance partner?"

She looked over at us and nodded, her silent gesture telling us that she had his back without making him feel like a baby. Of all the protectors we could have had for Jase, she was the best.

Jase nodded and let her lead him out onto the dance floor. It was funny that he now looked her in the eye. At this rate, he would be taller than her in a few more months.

Satisfied, Lance led me onto the dancefloor, too, while Sirena snuggled onto his shoulder. She was asleep as soon as Lance and I started swaying to the music.

"She's a daddy's girl." I smiled, rubbing her back as we danced.

Lance chuckled. "I'm enjoying it while it lasts."

"In a few more years, when she meets a boy—"

"Don't even say it," he cut me off. "I think I just may have to hire her a full-time bodyguard."

I burst out laughing, shaking my head. "Those poor boys. She won't be able to get a date to save her life. They'll all be too afraid of you."

"Good!" He smiled. "I want them to be! She's our little princess."

I nodded, leaning against Lance's shoulder when Amy approached and took her from him. "Okay, Daddy. I'll take her now."

He chuckled. "Thanks, Amy." Then he looked into my eyes as he wrapped his arms around my waist. "Now I can give Mama some time."

Amy rolled her eyes and then walked back to the table with Sirena sleeping on her shoulder.

I wrapped my arms around Lance's neck as he gazed into my eyes.

"How did I get so lucky to have you?" He took my hand and held it to his chest as he slid the other around my waist.

"Funny. I was just thinking the same thing about you." I looked into his eyes and smiled. "Happy Anniversary, darling."

"Happy Anniversary, love." Then his lips descended upon mine in a not-so-chaste kiss. Then he pulled back and leaned his head against mine.

We danced through that song and the next, and I didn't want this night to end. Lance and I had come a long way, but we made it here. I just hoped the rest of our lives could be like this.

Suddenly, Lance's head snapped up, searching the crowd. People around us smiled and offered their congratulations, and Lance and I nodded, thanking them. But there was something wrong.

"Lance, what is it?" I asked, looking into his eyes. "You don't have to protect me anymore. Tell me."

He shook his head, smiling. "Just saying goodbye to old ghosts."

But I knew my husband, and it was much more than that. I just hoped he told me what was going on before the ghost comes knocking on our door.

CHAPTER 2

Leila

Even though I knew that Lance wasn't telling me everything, it was our anniversary, and I didn't want to spoil it. I looked over, and Jase was still dancing with Addie.

"You know, Jase is a good dancer," I said, surprised.

Lance chuckled. "Yes, I think Addie's been teaching him when we're not looking. It looks like she wants to make sure he's got the moves when it's time for him to start dating."

I burst out laughing, shaking my head. "So, it's okay for Jase to date, but it's not okay for Sirena?"

Lance looked at me as if wondering what the problem was.

I smiled, shaking my head. "If Jase is allowed to date when he's old enough, then so will Sirena. We won't have different rules for each of our children. It's not fair. And keeping her on a tight leash will just make her turn wild."

Lance nodded, pulling me close as he leaned his head against mine. "Well, thank goodness we have a few more years before we have to start worrying about that." Then he raised his head and gazed into my eyes. "But if she's anything like her mother, she'll be a heartbreaker."

A smile lit my lips as I placed my hand on his cheek. "And if Jase is anything like his father, he will be suave, debonair, and a lady killer."

Lance laughed. "Well, let's hope not literally."

I chuckled, shaking my head. "Only you, Lance."

Then he leaned in close, giving me a sexy look. "Want to go upstairs?"

I nodded toward Jase. "Do you think he'll be okay here with Addie alone?"

Lance shook his head, his smile gone. "No. Tonight, I'm not letting him out of my sight."

"Amy will be here, Lance, and he's getting older—"

"No," he said a bit louder than I had expected him to.

I stopped dancing and looked into his eyes. "Lance, what's wrong? Tell me now, and don't sugarcoat it. You no longer have to protect me. And if there's danger, I need to know so I can protect our children. I've been working out with Kellen, Channing, and Lorenzo—"

"Leila, you don't know what you're saying." He clenched his jaw.

"Lance, tell me."

He stared into my eyes, debating. "Okay. But keep dancing and don't let on that anything's wrong." He bit his lower lip. "I had to kill Jeremy tonight."

"You what?" I stopped dancing and took a step back.

Lance looked around to see if anyone noticed and then took me into his arms again. "Leila, you promised."

I nodded, smiling at the people who were watching. When they went back to dancing, I turned to Lance. "Why? What happened?"

"I hated to have to do it, but when he was cutting my hair, he asked about you, wondering how you were doing." He let out a deep breath. "Then he started talking about you fighting off The Others in the cave with the knife from the C-section. After I said that I had never told him any of that and asked him how he knew, he tried to rake a straight razor across my throat."

I gasped. "You're kidding!"

"Shush!" He shook his head as he looked around. "Come to find out, he was a plant sent to infiltrate my coven years ago."

"My God...."

Lance nodded. "But before I killed him, I made him tell me who sent him."

I stopped dancing as I stared into his eyes. "Who was it?"

Lance let out a deep breath. "Raif."

"He's not after the cure for vampirism." Suddenly, it all made sense. "He's after our children, and it's personal."

Lance nodded. "I was afraid that the sins of my past would catch up with me one day, and it seems that they have."

"Lance, this isn't your fault." I shook my head. "Do not think for even one moment that this is your fault. Raif is crazy and just can't let the past go, but that's on him. Not you."

Lance nodded, letting out a deep breath. "I wish it were true, but I'm afraid I drove him to this long ago—"

"Stop. Stop that kind of talk right now. You went on with your life and let the past go. But it's obvious that he hasn't." I placed my hand on his cheek, forcing him to look at me. "But Lance, from here on out, you need to tell me when there's danger so I can protect the children and you, too."

"Leila, don't worry for one moment about me." He held my hand, forcing me to look into his eyes. "I am your husband, and it's my job to protect you and the children. It's not up to you—"

"Watch me," I said, cutting him off. "If anyone comes near my children, I'll attack and will ask questions later."

Lance smiled as he gently brushed his lips across mine. "That's my girl." Then he pulled me close, and we continued dancing. "Now you know why I haven't let the children out of my sight tonight."

I nodded, understanding. "But that's exactly why you need to tell me things like this. If I would have let Jase stay down here with Addie and Amy, and something happened to him, I'd never forgive myself."

Lance nodded. "Why don't you just let me do the worrying for both of us?"

I shook my head. "Lance, I don't want to argue. Let's just enjoy our anniversary. Okay?"

A smile lit his lips. "Speaking of our anniversary, I have reservations for us tomorrow night. But now, I'm not so sure we should go without the children."

I nodded, understanding. "We can do it another time, or we can bring the children with us."

Lance let out a deep breath. "Let's just play it by ear. But with Addie here, I could ask Amy to come over, too, and place bodyguards outside the door—"

"I think that'll be more than enough. Also, the children will be inside the castle." I let out a deep breath as we swayed to the music. "I just don't want to disrupt our lives any more than we have to. We can't live in fear."

Lance nodded as he ran the back of his hand gently over my cheek. "You never have to be afraid of anything with me here to protect you."

I bit my lower lip, wanting to word it correctly. "Lance, the only thing I'm afraid of is losing you and the kids."

He nodded, letting out a deep breath. "That's the only thing that scares me, too."

This time when he pulled me close, all talking stopped as we enjoyed being in the moment with each other. Time is fleeting, and none of us know how long we have... even immortals. When the song came to an end, we clapped and then walked off the floor.

"I think it's time to give Amy a break." I smiled, wanting to change the subject. "She might want to dance after all."

"Oh, she's fine." Lance chuckled. "I haven't seen her date in a while, although I'm not sure why."

"There you are." Amy smiled, keeping her voice low.

"How was she?" I asked as Lance lifted Sirena to his shoulder.

"She was great!" Amy shrugged. "Slept the whole time."

"And you promised me a dance." Lorenzo smiled as he held his hand out to her.

She laughed. "So, I did."

"Well, I thought I'd catch you before another man has a chance to steal you away." Lorenzo gave her a sexy smile as he offered her his arm.

She took it, obviously enjoying the attention. "Then what are we waiting for?"

He nodded to Lance and me as a smile lit his lips. "If you'll excuse us."

"Of course!" Lance stepped aside to let them pass.

I cleared my throat. "And what was it you said about Amy not dating in a while?"

Lance shrugged. "I stand corrected." Lance sat down with Sirena, and I took the seat beside him. "Let's wait until this song is over, and I'll ask Jase if he's ready to go."

I shook my head, enjoying watching him and Addie dance together. "No. I don't want to spoil his fun. Let him dance. We're in no hurry."

Lance nodded, following my gaze. "He's growing up quickly. Isn't he?"

I nodded, letting out a deep breath. "Too quickly."

Lance smiled as he slipped his arm around me. "So, did you ever think your life would turn out this way?"

I chuckled. "No. It's even better than I'd ever imagined, thanks to you." I tilted my head to the side, gazing into his eyes. "And did you ever imagine that your life would turn out this way?"

He burst out laughing. "Not in a million years." Then he leaned in close, his lips next to mine. "It's so much more, thanks to you."

I placed my hand gently on his cheek. "Happy anniversary, darling."

"Happy anniversary, love."

Then his lips descended upon mine in a not-so-chaste kiss, and I knew that everything we'd gone through to get here had been worth it.

"Lance, when you said you were saying goodbye to old ghosts, what did you mean by that?"

His smile faded, but he said nothing as he looked up at Jase and Addie, who were doing a version of the pretzel that Addie had obviously taught him, twisting around each other's arms, laughing.

"Lance, you promised."

He looked into my eyes. "I thought I saw Selestra."

My eyes nearly bugged out of my head. "Here?"

He nodded, giving me a reassuring smile. "But it was probably nothing."

"And what would it mean if she was here in the castle?" I shivered at the thought.

Lance let out a deep breath, his smile gone. "It wouldn't be good." He bit his lower lip. "I once saw her slaughter a village just for sport." Then his eyes met mine. "No, it wouldn't be good at all. Never underestimate her."

I nodded as a shiver ran up my spine. Lance didn't say it, but he didn't have to. If she was in the castle, we were as good as dead. But there was no way that I was going to let that happen.

"But don't worry." He smiled, shaking his head. "I haven't seen her again, so it was probably just my imagination playing tricks on me."

I raised my eyebrows as my eyes met his. "You will tell me, though, won't you? If you see her again?"

Lance let out a deep breath and then nodded. "Yes, I will." He chuckled. "Leila, you're going to have to be patient with me. I'm used to dealing with dangerous situations alone, so it's going to take a while to get used to telling you things."

I chuckled, nuzzling onto his arm. "Well, you'd better get used to it." Then my eyes met his. "Because you're not alone anymore."

He leaned in close and breathed against my lips. "And neither are you."

Then his lips crushed down onto mine, and I opened for him as passion overtook us both, not caring who saw us. Lance pulled back a moment later and licked his lips, smiling. "Well, love, unless you want me to take you right here in full view of our friends and family, I think it's time to go."

I burst out laughing. "Yeah, right! That would make a good impression, I'm sure."

Lance shrugged. "Free entertainment."

We both burst out laughing.

"Lance, promise me something."

He smoothed his hand over the side of my head, running his fingers through my hair. "Anything."

I placed my hand on his face as I gazed into his eyes. "Promise me that it'll always be like this between us."

But his smile faded, and his eyes were filled with so much love I thought my heart would burst receiving it. "I promise."

CHAPTER 3

Leila

A smile lit Angela's face as she approached our table. "Happy anniversary, you two!"

"Thank you," I replied, giving her a kind smile. "And thanks for setting up the decorations."

She chuckled, placing a hand on her chest. "Who, me?"

I laughed. "I'd know your style anywhere."

"Well, *ma cherie*, that's very kind of you to say," she said in her beautiful French accent and then reached over and gently squeezed our hands. "I wish you a long life filled with love." She started to walk away when Lance stopped her.

"Angela, do you have a minute?" He nodded toward a vacant chair across the table from us in a way that she couldn't say no to.

A crease formed between her eyes. "Yes, of course. What seems to be wrong?" She perched on the edge of the chair, her back straight in perfect posture.

Lance let out a deep breath as he rubbed Sirena's back. "I had to kill Jeremy tonight."

Her eyes widened. "What? Why?" She started to stand, but Lance held a hand up to stop her.

"Because he almost took my head off with a straight razor."

A crease formed between her eyes. "What happened?"

Lance told her everything just as he had told me as Angela listened intently. When he finished, he tilted his head to the side. "Jeremy was a plant sent to infiltrate my coven by Raif, someone I knew long ago. Do you know anything about that?"

Angela shook her head, her eyes filled with concern. "No. Not at all." She let out a deep breath as she looked down and then up again. "I'm sorry. It's just a lot to process. When you sent him to me,

I thought everything you told me about him was true. And over the years, he's never given me cause to doubt." She placed a hand on her cheek and then lowered it. "I'm so sorry, but I never imagined he'd ever turn on you like that."

Lance nodded, giving her a kind smile. "I know. I just wanted to speak with you about it to see if you noticed anything out of the ordinary."

She slowly shook her head, thinking. "No, not at all. He had his days off, like the rest of us. But he rarely left the castle." She let out a deep breath. "If he was feeding this Raif information, he did it when he was out."

Lance nodded, giving her a warm smile. "I know. Thank you for your help, Angela."

She nodded once. "If you'll excuse me...." Then she held a hand to her face as she left the room.

"I should go talk to her—"

But Lance grabbed my hand. "No. Give her some time to grieve." He looked into my eyes. "He's been a member of her team now for a long time."

I let out a deep breath. "I just hate that she had to find out this way."

He nodded. "Me, too, but I had no choice."

"Well, it looks as if we'll have to try and find Raif before he finds us." I looked over at Jase, but this time, he was dancing with another girl, and Addie was dancing with another man who was a foot taller than her. But she kept a close eye on Jase, watching his every move.

"I hate that Angela had to find out that way."

He nodded. "Me, too."

As we watched, the song ended, and Jase thanked the girl for the dance but then went straight back over to Addie. I was glad they got along so well. He couldn't have a better protector or friend.

Soon, Lance motioned for Jase and Addie to come over, and they did, laughing and clowning around. She was still young enough in spirit to have fun with him but old enough to set rules and boundaries, too. I was glad that she was such a good friend to Jase.

"Time to go, son," Lance said, rising to his feet.

"Ah, Dad!" Jase shook his head, but Addie rubbed his shoulder in a soothing motion.

"Son, your sister's been asleep for a while, and we have to get her to bed." Lance gave him a firm look that told him that it wasn't up for debate.

"Dad, could I just stay here with Addie for a while longer?" His eyes were hopeful.

"No, son," Lance replied. "It's time to say goodnight. You'll see Addie tomorrow."

Jase nodded, clearly disappointed. "Yes, sir."

I rubbed his shoulder. "We'll wait for you at the door." Then I pulled Addie in for a hug. "Thanks for everything. We'll see you tomorrow."

She nodded when I released her. "I'll be there." Then she looked over at Jase. "I'll see you tomorrow."

He nodded, smiling. "See ya."

Then she headed off to join a group of her friends but waved to Jase once more when we left.

"So, did you have a good time tonight, son?" I asked as we stepped into the elevator.

He nodded, smiling. "Addie knows all kinds of dances! She's so fun."

I chuckled, looking up at Lance as he smiled, listening.

"Yes, Dad and I saw you two doing the Pretzel!" I laughed, shaking my head. "That's always fun."

Jase laughed. "Yeah, we were twisting so many ways it was hard for me to keep up at first, but then I got the hang of it."

The doors opened, and we stepped out into the hallway and were in our penthouse a few moments later.

"Night, Jase." Lance smiled as he headed toward the right where the children's rooms were to put Sirena down.

"Jase, don't be angry that we left." I pulled him in for a hug. "It was for a reason."

Jase nodded when I released him. "It's okay, Mom. Have a good night."

"Would you like for me to tuck you in?" I asked, my eyes hopeful.

He scrunched up his nose. "Mom! Really? I'm old enough to tuck myself in now."

I nodded, smiling. "So you are." I leaned down and kissed his cheek. "I love you, son."

"Love you, too, Mom." He yawned as he headed down the hallway toward his bedroom. But halfway down the hallway, Lance met him when he came out and gently squeezed his shoulder as he walked with him to his room.

I checked on Sirena, and she was sound asleep, all covered over. Then I leaned on the door facing of Jase's room, watching. But they were having a manly talk, so I walked discretely away, giving them time alone.

I headed into our room and sat on the edge of the bed to take off my shoes. Then I put them away in the closet. Since I was a vampire, I got tired occasionally, but it was a different kind of tired. Physically, I was strong enough to demolish a whole building. But it was more of an emotional tiredness when I needed to recharge.

Just then, Lance walked in the door, looking at me with hungry eyes.

"Are the children—"

I didn't get to finish the sentence when his lips slammed into mine, and he scooped me into his arms, never breaking the kiss. His lips groped mine hungrily, and I bit his lower lip and then crushed my lips to his as he carried me to the bed, looking down at me like a starving man looking at water.

I slid my hands up his chest, feeling his muscled chest as I unbuttoned his shirt. He slid his hands down my sides, causing my breath to quicken as I looked into his deep, green eyes. It didn't matter how many times Lance had touched me, each time was electric.

"Seeing you in that dress, I've wanted to fuck you all night." He gripped the hem of my dress and pulled it up over my head, then flung it to the floor, leaving me only in my bra, panties, and high heels. "You are one gorgeous woman," he breathed, kissing my neck. I arched my back as tingles shot all over my body.

"You are so sexy," I breathed, pushing him onto the bed as I ran my hands over his muscled chest and kissed his chest. "Happy anniversary, darling."

He lifted up, and a mischievous grin spread across his lips as he kissed the tender skin between my breasts. "I'm ready for my present now." He ran his hands up my body, undid my bra with a flick of his wrist, then slid it off and threw it onto the floor.

Tingles spread over my body as he breathed against my skin, going straight to my sex. "Oh? And what present is that?"

Lance rolled me over onto my back, smiling as he looked up. "You."

He kissed down my body to my breasts, tonguing my nipple as he sucked, and then went to the other side, causing my breath to quicken under his touch. Then he moved lower, kissing my stomach as his hands slid down my sides and then under me, gripping my ass while his mouth moved down, making me pant under his touch. He smiled up at me, and then bit the sides of my panties and pulled them off with his teeth, exposing my sex.

"God, you're gorgeous...." His eyes combed my body, making me feel every inch a queen as he kissed down my leg and then slipped off one shoe, smiling as he looked into my eyes. Then he kissed down the other, taking off my other shoe, ticking my foot with just a touch as the shoe hit the floor. Wrapping his arms around my legs, he grabbed my ass and pulled me to him as he kissed down my legs, closer to my heat, my heart pounding in anticipation.

Then his mouth was on my heat, and I gasped, closing my eyes. His tongue darted over my clit as I pushed against him.

"Fuck me, Lance," I breathed. "I want to feel you inside me... now."

He smiled against my pussy. "In a minute. Be patient," his voice rumbled against my heat, causing me to want him more. "Just relax."

I closed my eyes and leaned back, enjoying his hands gripping my ass as his tongue darted in and out, fucking me with his tongue as I pushed against his mouth, wanting more. He ran his fingers along my skin as his tongue worked its magic, darting in and out faster until I could feel or hear or see nothing but him. I moaned as his tongue went deeper inside until I exploded in orgasm, moaning his name over and again.

Satisfied, he trailed kisses across my skin and up my body, stroking his cock as precum leaked out. Then he pushed into me a moment later, causing me to gasp as his lips crashed down onto mine. His tongue swiped over mine, letting me taste myself on him as he fucked me.

I closed my eyes and leaned back, but he grabbed my throat, forcing me to look at him as he rolled into me, genuinely making love to me. Then he pushed faster and harder, his breaths coming quicker as his blood called to me. I rolled him over, and he wrapped his arms tightly around me, fucking me sensually.

Unable to take any more, I bared my fangs and sank them into his neck as he moaned in pleasure. His luscious blood rushed into my mouth and down my throat as he leaned his head back, letting me take my fill. My walls clenched around him, causing his length to swell as he moved faster into me, moaning my name as he pulled me tightly to him until he threw his head back, moaning in ecstasy as we found release together.

I kissed his neck as he caught his breath. "You've been holding out on me." I smiled against his neck, moving down to his muscled chest.

"What?" he asked, barely coherent, enjoying the afterglow.

"While I was human...." I tongued his nipple and then down to his stomach, smiling as I looked up at him. "You were holding back."

"Sweetheart, I had to." He quickly flipped me over and slid my legs over his shoulders, pushing into me again. "If I took you as hard as I plan to now, I would have killed you."

I chuckled. "Well, it's a good thing you didn't then."

All talking stopped as he pushed into me, harder and faster until only the sound of our skin pounding together and our moans were audible in the room. Then I arched my back, raising toward him, meeting each of his thrusts with one of my own, until his cock swelled inside me, sending me over the edge as he exploded inside me, sending warmth throughout my sex.

"God, I love you," I breathed, never wanting this moment to end.

"I love you more." A mischievous smile lit his lips as he bit my ankle and sucked my blood while still inside me, causing my heat to rise again. Blood sharing was intimate, one of the most erotic things vampires could do. When he had his fill, he licked the wound, and it immediately healed, but he was far from done.

He slid my leg over his shoulder and let the other one down, pushing into me over and again as I moaned, slamming into me until his cock swelled, sending me over the edge. My walls clamped down hard around him as we climaxed together... and Raif and Selestra coming after us were the farthest things from my mind. But the way I felt at this moment, let them come. Like Lance, I would do anything to protect what's mine.

CHAPTER 4

Lance

Faint rays of morning sunshine peeked through the windows the following morning as I turned over and kissed Leila's shoulder, causing her to wake.

"Lance?" She smiled, her eyes half-mast.

"Yes, it's me, love." I rolled over and kissed her lips. "Go back to sleep. I'm going to take a shower."

She turned over and smiled, curling up on her pillow—an angel sent down from Heaven just for me. What a wonderful sight to wake up to.

I slipped on some sleeping shorts in case the children woke and headed out to the kitchen. After making the coffee, I threw two blood bags into the microwave, took them out when they were ready, and headed to the door to get the paper. When I opened it, Channing and Javier were standing outside.

"Good morning, sir." Channing nodded, smiling as he handed me the newspaper.

"Thank you." After taking the paper, I gave them the blood bags. "Here you go, gentlemen."

"Thank you, sir." Javier smiled as he drank down his and then handed the empty pouch back to me.

"When is the next shift coming to relieve you?" There was no way that I'd expect my men to be on their shift longer than was necessary.

"Two men are coming to relieve us soon." Channing handed me his empty bag, too.

"I want someone on guard outside this door around the clock until further notice." I made a mental note to speak with Ferdinand, my head of security, about it soon.

"Yes, sir," Javier replied. "Ferdinand has guards assigned here around the clock until further notice."

I nodded, clasping his shoulder. "Thank you." When I went back inside, Leila was sitting at the table with two long-stemmed glasses filled with blood and two cups of coffee at our place settings. "Well, good morning, beautiful! I'm sorry if I woke you."

She shook her head, swirling the blood in the glass, and then took a sip. "No, I needed to get up anyway. I want to speak with Amy about the new wing of Drake's building today. She and Elias have been heading up the clinic for the transformations, so I'm sure they have their hands full."

I sat at the table and looked at her over my paper. "You're not thinking of going back to work already. Are you?"

Leila shook her head, smiling. "No, I just thought I'd check in and see if there was anything I could do to help." She shrugged as she stood and wrapped her arms around my neck. "And since you were already going in—"

"You thought you'd tag along." In one fluid motion, I wrapped my arms around her waist and pulled her onto my lap. "Keep doing that, and I may not let you out of the house for a month."

She leaned in close, looking into my eyes. "Promises, promises."

I pushed her beautiful blonde hair back away from her face and crushed my lips to hers. She opened for me as I deepened the kiss. Then all too soon, she pulled back and gave me one last sweet kiss.

"I'll leave you to your paper." Then she rose to her feet, headed over to the stove, and pulled out a pan. "So, what would you like for breakfast?"

I shrugged, paging through my paper. "Whatever you want is fine with me." Even though most people nowadays get their news from the Internet, I still prefer my morning newspaper. Call me old-fashioned, but there was something about the smell of the ink and getting lost in the print and articles that had me hooked.

Leila looked over her shoulder. "Biscuits and sausage gravy?"

I nodded, smiling. "Sounds good."

I had wanted a human life for so long, but this was close to it. Even though we were vampires, we tried to carry on with our lives as normally as possible. Not only for the children, but for ourselves, as well.

Many a vampire got sucked into the darker parts of this life, and that's not what I wanted for my family, and neither did Leila. Even though we were far from being a normal family, we wanted a good home life for our children.

I drank the blood and my coffee as I perused the paper. When I finished, I folded it and set it in the bin next to the desk on the wall to be recycled. Then I wrapped my arms around Leila's waist and kissed her neck. "I'm going to take a shower. Want to join me?"

A smile lit her lips. "I would, but the children will be up soon, and I want to make them breakfast before we go." She arched an eyebrow. "Raincheck?"

"Absolutely."

Later that morning, I smiled at Leila as I held the limo door open for her. She was a queen, and I intended to treat her like one for the rest of our lives.

When we were ready, Charles, our driver, pulled out of the parking lot headed toward Southside Medical Hospital.

Leila gave my hand a gentle squeeze, claiming my attention, a worried look in her eyes. "Are you sure the children will be okay while we're away?" she asked for the hundredth time.

I kissed her hand and wrapped my arm around her, pulling her to my side. "Leila, they'll be fine. Don't worry. Michael and George are standing guard outside, and Addie is there with them, too."

"I think we should get another babysitter for Sirena." She sighed as she looked out the window, watching the scenery pass. "That way, both she and Jase will have bodyguards."

I nodded, letting out a deep breath. "I was thinking the same thing. But right now, Adeline doesn't seem to mind watching them both. And with the bodyguards outside, the children will have plenty of protection."

"I hope you're right."

I placed my finger under her chin and turned her face to mine. "You know I am. I've also strengthened the number of guards around the castle, so they'll be fine. Also, we're not going to be gone long."

She lifted her eyebrows. "Promise?"

I kissed the tip of her nose, smiling at her innocent look. "I promise." Soon, we pulled into the hospital parking lot. "Pull around back. Will you, Charles?"

He nodded, his eyes meeting mine in the rearview mirror. "Yes, of course, sir." Leila looked up at me, wondering why we were going toward the back. "I don't want to take long today." I raised her hand to my lips and kissed it. "Since we're out alone, I thought maybe we could do something."

"Like what?" She smiled. "Are we still going out tonight?"

I nodded, enjoying her reaction. She hated surprises, and I always loved giving them to her. "Yes, but we could do something before we go home. Like, take a walk at the Hoover Dam?"

She laughed. "I'm not dressed for a long trek."

Since she became a vampire, we'd been taking runs through the Oasis or the desert, leaping over river gorges, and more.

I laughed. "No, I just mean a regular walk, but we can see how we feel later."

The driver slid the car into park, and he and the two guards opened our doors a moment later. Maybe I was going a little overboard with security, but I wasn't taking any chances with my family.

I walked around the car and placed my hand on the small of her back. Her cream-colored dress looked exquisite and showed off her womanly curves in all the right places. The back had a diamond cutout, and she wore cream strappy heels. I was surprised that she dressed up today just to come to the hospital. But since she was no longer working here, it didn't really matter. She could wear anything she wanted, and I loved the way she dressed.

"Would you like me to go upstairs with you?" I asked when we stopped at the private elevator.

She shook her head, smiling. "No, I'll be fine. You go ahead. Just come and get me when you're ready."

I nodded, giving her one last sweet kiss. "I will. If you need me, just call."

I waited with her until she was safely in the elevator, and she wiggled her fingers goodbye, leaving me to feel like the luckiest man in the world.

"There you are!" Drake said behind me. I turned around, and my blood turned cold. "Lance, I'd like you to meet our newest patron, Silvia Gold."

"Well, hello, Lance. It's been a while." Her reddish-brown hair waved over her shoulders, and she wore a red silk dress and high heels.

Growling loudly and baring my teeth, I quickly closed the distance between us, grabbed her by the throat, and slammed her against the wall.

"Lance! What the hell do you think you're doing?" Drake yelled. "Silvia has become an important patron to the hospital!"

"Like hell she is!" I yelled, pushing her down the hallway by the throat, never taking my eyes from hers. "We need a private room! Now!"

"Lance, let her go!" Drake yelled. "What the hell is wrong with you?"

"Her name is Selestra!" I yelled, walking her down the hallway, never easing my hold on her throat. "She's my ex, and she's been stalking my family and me!"

Selestra didn't look affected and didn't try to fight me. "Well, well! It looks like I've hit a nerve."

Drake hurried around us, flung open the door, and quickly flipped on the light. "Now, what the hell is going on here?"

I ignored him. Instead, I threw her into the room and locked the door behind us. "What the hell are you doing here, Selestra? You stalked my wife in Paris while she was pregnant, for God's sake!"

She shrugged, folding her arms across her chest. "I was curious."

"Curious?" I threw a chair against the wall out of my way and headed toward her. "Curious? My wife was pregnant and human, and you were *curious?*" I grabbed her by the throat again, but this time, she threw me over her shoulder, and I landed flat on my back on the table. She was straddling me a moment later. I flipped her over my head, and her back crashed hard against the wall. I was on my feet and headed toward her within a second.

"Enough!" Drake yelled, stepping between us. "This is a hospital, for heaven's sake!"

I pointed my finger at her. "You're lucky I don't tear you apart!"

"You will do no such thing!" Drake yelled.

I pinned him against the wall by the throat without a second thought.

But he looked me in the eye, arching an eyebrow. "Lance, do you really want to go there?"

I growled and released him. "She's been stalking my family, Drake!" I shook my head, trying to calm down. "She and Raif told The Outsiders that my son's blood was the cure for vampirism! And you want me to calm down?"

"Yes." Drake glared at me. Then his head snapped up toward her. "What the hell do you think you're doing, stalking Lance and his family like that?"

She shrugged, slinking toward me, and stopped, folding her arms over her chest. "I wanted to see the woman who stole your heart." She scoffed. "Color me surprised when I found out she was human." Selestra took a deep breath while circling me and then ran her finger along my shoulder and down my arm. "But last night, I saw that she's a vampire now. At least she's on equal footing with me now."

"She's nothing like you!" I grabbed her arm, twisted it behind her back, and pushed her away, causing her to stumble on her high heels, but she quickly regained her balance. Then I turned to Drake. "Her name is Selestra, and she's my ex-girlfriend and one of the most manipulative, ruthless vampires he's ever known."

Selestra chuckled. "Why, thank you!"

"It wasn't a compliment." I let out a deep breath and glanced over at Drake, never taking my eyes from hers. "Be careful with her, Drake. She's a manipulator and likes to play games with men."

Selestra's smile faded. "I just can't understand why you'd want to be with her when you can have me."

I closed the distance between us, never taking my eyes from hers. "Because she's everything you're not."

"Oh?" Selestra smirked. "Even though she's a vampire now?"

"Enough!" Drake let out a deep breath, shaking his head. "Lance, let her go."

"Let her go?" My head snapped up as rage filled my chest. "She's been stalking my family, Drake, and you just want me to let her go?" My voice rose several octaves. Then my eyes returned to hers as one corner of my lips curled into a smile. "I'm going to hold her for judgment."

"No, you won't because she's done nothing wrong here. So, you're going to let her go." Drake stalked toward Selestra and looked her straight in the eye. "But if you go near Lance, his wife, or his family again, I'll kill you myself. Then he pointed toward the door. "Now, get out! And I never want to see you near this hospital again!"

She huffed and then walked out.

"Leila!" I ran out of the room, and Selestra was already gone. I just hoped she wasn't headed for Leila. If she even went near her again, I'd kill her. I don't care what Drake said.

Knowing the stairs were quicker, I sprinted up them as quickly as possible, taking two at a time, and threw open the door on Amy's floor, hoping I wasn't too late. Then I ran toward Amy's lab and flung the door open so hard it slammed into the wall.

Amy and Leila looked up, both immediately on their feet.

"Lance, what's wrong?" Leila asked, looking in my eyes from across the room.

"Get your things," I growled. "We're going."

"Lance?" Leila grabbed her purse and quickly crossed the room to me. "What happened?"

"I'll tell you on the way." I pulled her out, not giving Amy a second glance.

On the way downstairs to the limo, my eyes darted around, ensuring she wouldn't attack, catching us off guard.

"Lance, did something happen with the kids?"

I quickly shook my head. "No."

Downstairs, I pushed open the back door, and our limo and men were waiting outside. They quickly opened the doors, and we were on our way a few moments later.

"Okay, Lance." Leila glared at me. "What's going on?"

When my eyes met hers, I said only one word, "Selestra."

CHAPTER 5

Leila

"Did you see her here at the hospital?" If Selestra was running around and she approached him, I needed to know.

Lance nodded, his hands clenched into fists at his sides, but said nothing.

"Lance! Tell me!" I shouted. "I have to know!

He shook his head as he looked into my eyes. "Trust me. You don't want to know."

In the back of the limo, I placed my hand on his cheek to calm him as I looked into his eyes. "Lance, please. I have to know."

He let out a deep breath as he pulled me to his side. "As soon as we got there, Drake introduced me to a new patron of the hospital, Silvia Gold." He let out a deep breath, shaking his head. "Then, when I looked up, it was Selestra."

"Oh my God!" I gasped. "What did you do?"

He shrugged. "I grabbed her by the throat and took her to a room along with Drake." He shook his head. "Then I told her if she ever came near you, the children, or me again, I would kill her."

"So, where is she now?" Selestra was lucky that Lance hadn't ripped her heart out right then and there.

Lance pursed his lips together. "I wanted to hold her for judgment with the Tribunal, but Drake persuaded me to let her go."

"What? Why?" But I quickly calmed myself, knowing Lance would do anything to protect his family.

He nodded as he turned to look into my eyes. "Drake said that she hadn't done anything there, so he insisted I let her go, and that's when I turned on him and nearly ripped out his throat."

"Seriously?" I shook my head, knowing Lance would never forgive himself if he killed Drake. "What did he do?"

"He asked me if I really wanted to go there... to fight with him." Lance shook his head. "Suffice it to say that I warned him about her and to be careful, and Drake told her that if she ever came near you, the kids, or me again, he'd kill her himself."

I nodded, understanding. "If she was smart enough to infiltrate the hospital, she could be anywhere. We'll have to be careful."

Lance's head snapped up. "Leila, she was in the castle last night. I thought I saw her briefly at our party and then brushed it off. But today, she confirmed she was there." He took my hand as he looked into my eyes. "Leila, she's been stalking you."

"What?" My blood ran cold at the thought.

Lance nodded. "In Paris when room service came, it was her. Also, she knew you were human then, and she knows you're a vampire now. So, she's been watching you."

"And if she's been watching me, she's been watching the kids and you." I let out a deep breath. "Lance, the children!"

He pulled out his cell phone and quickly dialed a number. "Adeline, are the children okay?"

"Yes, they're fine," she said on the other end. With my vampire hearing, I could hear Addie on the other end clearly. "Why? What's wrong?"

"Nothing." He let out a deep breath. "Just keep the children in the penthouse. There are guards outside the door, so don't worry. But if anyone comes to the door, do not let them in until we get there, no matter who they are."

"Yes, sir," she replied on the other end.

"If you need us, call me right away."

"Yes, of course." He hung up a moment later. "Thank goodness, the children are safe." He gave me a small smile. "I'm sorry we have to rush right back."

I sighed, shaking my head. "Lance, don't worry about that at all. I'm glad you told me."

Lance shook his head, his eyes reluctantly meeting mine. "Leila, it's my job to protect you and the children—"

"And you do," I cut him off. "I'm glad you told me so I can keep a lookout for her, too, now that I know what she looks like." I remembered all too clearly the woman who had posed as room service in Paris when I was human, pregnant, and alone. "What does she want?"

His lips formed a straight line as he looked into my eyes. "Me."

I scoffed. "You mean to tell me that she's been stalking the kids and me because she wants you?"

He nodded. "When I asked her why she came near you while you were pregnant, she said she was 'curious.'" He scoffed, shaking his head.

"Curious?" My head snapped up. "About me?"

"About why I would want you when I could have her." He shook his head in disgust. "I told her you were nothing like her." His eyes met mine. "I also told her I'd kill her if she came near you or the children again. In fact, I should have killed her right then and there as soon as I saw her at the hospital."

I shook my head, rubbing his arm in a soothing motion. "No, you did the right thing. You're not a murderer."

His eyes turned cold. "If it means protecting you and the children, then yes, I am."

The limo pulled down the long drive of Caprice Casino.

"Pull up out front," Lance ordered.

"Yes, sir." Usually, Lance had the driver go to our private entrance in the back, but not this time.

Lance gave my hand a gentle squeeze and kissed it. "Leila, I'm so sorry about this. But I promise you. I'll make this right."

"I know." I touched his cheek as my lips curled into a smile. "Just promise me you'll never leave me for her."

He chuckled. "Love, get that thought out of your mind right now. There's no comparison between the two of you. Also, you have my heart, now and always."

I nodded, smiling.

"But promise me that you'll never leave me, either." He shook his head, his smile fading. "I couldn't bear it if another man stole you away from me."

I smiled, looking into his eyes. "Lance, that'll never happen. You're it for me. I never want anyone else but you."

He wrapped me in his arms and pulled me to his chest, inhaling my scent. Then his lips descended upon mine, his lips saying what his voice couldn't. A moment later, he pulled back, concern filling his eyes. "Leila, just promise me you'll be careful. Both Raif and Selestra are manipulative, and they're both out to destroy me. And if Selestra came on to me today, I'm afraid Raif will try to do the same with you... and he's a very handsome man."

"And so are you. But that's not why I'm with you."

He looked into my eyes.

I pressed my hand to his chest and smiled. "Lance, you have the biggest heart of anyone I know." Then I placed my hand on his cheek. "You have nothing to worry about."

The driver pulled the car to a stop in front of Caprice Casino a moment later. Lance was out before the driver could open his door, and I was right behind him. He placed his hand on the small of my back as we walked inside.

"Ferdinand, I want the castle secure," Lance ordered as soon as we walked in. "There was a breach here last night."

Ferdinand nodded once. "Yes, sir. We'll check everyone who enters and leaves."

"And I want every exit secured," Lance ordered as we headed toward the elevator. "I don't care if you have to deadbolt them from the inside."

The doors opened on the top floor a moment later, and two guards were standing outside our door.

"Has anyone entered or left since we've been gone?" Lance asked as I opened the door.

"No, sir," they both said in unison.

Lance continued barking orders as I rushed into the penthouse, and down the hallway to the family room. Jase was sitting on a chair with his leg slung over the armrest, reading a book, while Sirena played with her doll on the floor.

Addie was on her feet immediately. "Is everything okay?"

I nodded, my eyes darting to the children, and she nodded once, understanding.

"Mom?" Jase looked up from his book and sat up, putting his foot down on the floor. "Is something wrong?"

I shook my head, giving him a reassuring smile. "Everything's fine, dear. You just stay in here with Addie while I talk to Dad for a minute. Okay?"

Jase pursed his lips, reminding me of his father. Even though he had my coloring, he looked so much like Lance it was uncanny.

"Mom...." He quickly crossed the room to me, his voice merely a whisper. "Sirena is still too young to know, but you can tell me if something's going on. I'm old enough now—"

"I know, son." I kissed his forehead, knowing that soon he'd be too tall for me to do that. "But everything's fine. Go on back to your reading."

From the expression on his face, he wasn't buying it. But he pressed his lips together and nodded once as he went back to his book.

"I know!" Addie piped up. "Let's play a game of Chess. Shall we?"

Jase nodded as he headed toward a wooden table in the corner to set up the chessboard.

"I'll play, too!" Sirena chimed in.

"Okay. Come on, Sirena." Jase took her by the hand, glaring at me as he led her toward the Chess set. "You can play with me against Addie."

"Yeah!" Sirena clapped as they settled in for a game.

Jase sat down and pulled her onto his lap, still glaring at me when Lance walked in.

"How are the children?"

"Dad, I'm no longer a child." Jase looked up, glaring at him, too.

"You're my child." Lance let out a deep breath, collecting himself. Then he crossed the room to the kids and kissed the top of their heads.

To my surprise, Jase didn't object. "Dad, you can tell me what's going on—"

"Not now, son," Lance cut him off, then smiled as he stroked his hair. "Protect your sister and stay with Adeline. Now that you're becoming a man in this house, you'll have to start looking out for your little sister. As men, we must protect the women at all cost." Lance smiled down at Jase. "That can be your job. Okay? When Mom, Addie, and I aren't with you, you'll need to protect your sister."

Jase nodded, smiling up at him with adoration. "Okay, Dad."

Lance ruffed his hair. "That's my boy!"

"Dad!" Jase blushed, pulling away, and turned his attention toward the game, taking special care to explain how to play Chess to Sirena.

"He's growing up fast." Lance shook his head as we walked into the living room, leaving them to their game.

"Too fast." I smiled up at him. "You handled that very well, by the way."

Lance smiled. "Well, I remember being that age. He wants to grow up but doesn't quite know how to do it yet. So, giving him a job will be good for him. Also, he needs to look out for his sister in the event that we can't."

I nodded. "I hate the thought of Jase having so much responsibility at his age."

Lance smiled as he leaned in and kissed my forehead. "He'll be fine. It'll be good for him. Besides, I will be there to protect them both, so there's no need to worry."

"I'll be there, too. Lance, I've been training—"

"Leila, if it ever comes down to a fight, I don't want you mixed up in it," Lance cut me off. "You'll stay with the children, and I'll do what needs to be done."

"But I'll need to know how to fight to protect the children, too." I sighed, shaking my head.

He pulled me into his arms and kissed the top of my head. "Yes, but no matter what happens, your priority is to protect the children."

I nodded, understanding. Lance was right. Protecting the children was my first priority. In fact, that was one of the reasons why I wanted to become a vampire.

Lance's phone rang, and he quickly checked to see who was calling.

"Raven, what's wrong?" Lance looked into my eyes as he spoke.

"Nothing yet," she said from the other end. "But we need to talk."

"What about?"

There was a pause at the other end. "The children."

Lance nodded, even though she couldn't see him. "Leila's here. I'll put you on speakerphone."

"No need," she replied. "I'm right downstairs."

"I'll be right down." Lance clicked off as he looked into my eyes. "I'll be right back. Raven is right downstairs."

I nodded. "Of course."

When he was gone, I popped two blood bags into the microwave and called down to the kitchen for the chef to bring us up something special for Raven. It was lunchtime, and I was sure that the children hadn't eaten anything yet.

I emptied the contents of the blood bags into two long-stemmed glasses and then prepared three more for Adeline and the children, knowing the children probably hadn't had any yet today.

I emptied Sirena's into a sippy cup but prepared Jase's just like ours. If he was growing up, it was high time I started letting him.

Then I set Addie's and the children's glasses on a tray and took them down the hallway.

"Umm... that smells good!" Sirena took the cup I offered her and started downing it quickly.

"Here you go, Addie." I handed a glass to her and then looked at my son, who was frowning up at me. "This one is yours." His eyes lit up. "I've decided that since you're growing up, it's high time I let you."

"Thanks, Mom." He nodded, smiling, obviously glad that I was starting to notice that he was growing up.

I kissed the top of his head and then Sirena's. "I just ordered us some lunch, and Aunt Raven will be eating with us."

"Aunt Raven's here?" Jase's eyes lit up along with Sirena's. The children loved her. "But I thought she lived in New York."

I nodded, smiling. "She does, but she came for a surprise visit. Keep playing, drink your blood, and I'll let you know when lunch is ready."

I motioned with my head for Adeline to follow me. We walked down the hallway a safe distance from the children, and I stopped. "Raven's visit is rather unexpected. Would you mind staying for the rest of today to watch the children?"

She shook her head, scrunching up her eyebrows. "No! Not at all. I'd be glad to."

"Thank you." Then my smile faded. "Addie, there's something else I'd like to speak with you about, too."

"Oh?" she asked, taking a sip from her glass. "What's that?"

"We're thinking of hiring a bodyguard and babysitter for Sirena, too." I let out a deep breath. "Or are you good with both of the children alone for now?"

She thought for a moment. "Let's see how it goes. Usually, I wouldn't think twice about watching and protecting both of the children. But after the attack when Sirena was born, it would be nice to have someone else reliable here to help me protect them, just in case." She shrugged. "But on days like this, it wouldn't be a problem at all."

I took a sip of my blood and swallowed. "Thank you for your honesty. I'll let you know what we decide. But if you need anything, let me know."

She nodded, a smile lighting her lips. "I will."

When she turned and walked down the hallway toward the

children, I just hoped we could find Raif and Selestra soon, so this nightmare could end.

CHAPTER 6

Lance

I quickly hit the elevator button and was on the first floor within minutes. As soon as the doors opened, I looked across the casino, and Raven was there, wearing a long, green velvet cloak, attracting the attention of the humans in the casino. But I didn't care. Over the years, she had helped me more times than I could count. And now, she was helping Leila and the children, too. She was like family.

"Raven, it's so good of you to come!" I placed my hands on her shoulders and kissed both of her cheeks. "But I wish I would have known you were coming."

She gave me a small smile, her eyes filled with concern. "I'm sorry to drop in on you like this, but I assure you. It's important."

"Of course." I offered her my arm. "Shall we?"

She brought down the hood of her cloak and took my arm as her bodyguards followed. I went with her in the elevator while her men took the stairs, leaving us alone.

"Is something wrong?" I asked, my eyes filled with concern.

A smile lit her lips. "Let's wait until Leila is present. Shall we?"

I nodded as my heart fell. "Yes, of course." I knew Raven, and she wouldn't have come all this way unless she had a good reason, and I feared it involved my family. Or else why would she have popped in unannounced all the way from New York? I was just glad that I had been here when she arrived.

"Is everything okay in New York?" I asked when the elevator doors opened.

Her men were already standing outside the penthouse, chatting with the guards outside my door.

"All is well," she replied and then turned to one of her men when we approached. "Jim, will you and Franco stay out here, please?"

"Yes, mistress." He gave her a slight bow and stood back, waiting.

"Right this way." I opened the door for her and closed the door behind us. "May I take your cloak?"

"Yes. Thank you." She folded it after she took it off and handed it to me.

I took it to the coat closet to hand it up. "Raven, please make yourself comfortable. Leila's probably with the children now. She'll be right out."

A smile lit her lips. "May I see the children, if you don't mind?"

I chuckled. "Yes, of course. Right this way. They were excited when we told them you were here." I placed my hand on her shoulder and guided her down the hallway toward the family room.

"Lance, I love what you've done with the place!" Raven gushed, looking around. "This is a great addition and joins the rest of the penthouse seamlessly."

"Thank you. Riccardo is absolutely wonderful."

Raven arched an eyebrow as a smile lit her lips. "If you're not careful, I may have to steal him from you."

I laughed. "You can try."

"Raven!" Leila gently squeezed her hands as she gave her air kisses over both cheeks. "I'm so glad you came! But we wish we would have known. Please say that you'll stay a few days so we can visit."

A smile spread across Raven's face. "I'll stay the night if you don't mind, but I can't stay long."

"Of course," Leila replied. "You're always welcome. Stay as long as you like."

Then Raven spotted Jase, and her eyes great wide. "This isn't Jase, is it?"

A broad smile spread across his face as he took his sister's hand and led her over to Raven. "It's good to see you, Aunt Raven!" He pulled her in for a hug.

Raven didn't have to bend over much to hug him. "And this is Sirena? It's so good to see you both! My, my! You're growing so quickly!"

"Tell me about it." I laughed, shaking my head. "Before long, he'll be as tall as me."

"I'm almost as tall as Addie now!" he replied.

Adeline laughed. "That's not saying much."

Everyone laughed.

"Auntie Raven!" Sirena threw her arms around her, and Raven bent down to her level. "How's New York?"

Raven's eyes opened wide. "It's fine, thank you!" Raven looked up at Leila, and she nodded, smiling proudly.

Raven smiled. "As you said, they're growing too fast."

"Well, shall we?" I asked, gesturing toward the hallway.

Raven nodded. "Jase, Sirena, it's good to see you again."

"Addie, I ordered a big lunch for all of us," Leila said, her voice low. "I'll let you know when it arrives."

Adeline nodded. "Jase, Sirena? Let's finish our game. Okay?"

Raven watched as they took their places back at the Chess table. Then she walked out with us. "They're playing Chess already?"

I laughed. "Yes, and Jase will give you a run for your money. Sirena's just starting to learn, but Jase's been teaching her."

"You have a good nanny." Raven smiled as she entered the living room with us.

"Would you like a glass of wine?" Leila asked, heading toward the kitchen as Raven and I sat in the living room.

Raven took her usual seat on the sofa, and I sat on the club chair kitty-corner from her. Leila came in with a serving tray with a bottle of wine and long-stemmed wine glasses.

"I'll pour the wine." I smiled as I reached for the bottle and started pouring. "You two enjoy each other's company."

"I wish this were a social call." Raven sighed, taking the glass I offered. "But I'm here to discuss the children."

Leila's head snapped up as she took the glass I gave her. "What about them? Are they in danger?"

Raven nodded. "Yes, they are."

I took my wine and sat back down. "What did you see?"

Raven took a sip of her wine and then set it on the table. "What I'm about to say will be hard to hear, but it's imperative that you hear me out."

"Tell us." I closed the short distance between Leila and me and sat on the arm of the sofa, sliding my arm around her.

"I need you to let me take the children to New York for training and for their own protection."

"Absolutely not!" Leila shook her head but quickly calmed

herself. "We can protect them here."

I nodded, a crease forming between my eyes. "I agree. We would give our lives to keep our children safe."

Raven nodded. "Yes, I know, but it won't be enough."

"Why?" I sat on the club chair closest to Leila, leaning forward as I listened, the wine forgotten.

"There are people after your children. And if they come with me to my coven, they can begin their training." Raven let out a deep breath. "They can undergo their training at my Compound. And when they're old enough, they can go to Mayfield Manor for Magical Misfits."

"Magical Misfits?" I scrunched up my nose. "My children are not misfits."

Raven shrugged. "They are in society with the humans. Hence, the name. As witch-vampire hybrids, they need special training. With me or at the school, they can hone their skills while cultivating their understanding of other species. Also, they will have the opportunity to make friends like themselves."

Leila chuckled. "Well, I doubt there'll be other children quite like them."

"Which is why you need to consider it." Raven let out a deep breath. "Your children are special and will be the key to uniting the species. People were after them before they were born and will continue to come after them unless they receive training."

My eyes met Leila's, but she shook her head slightly. "Raven, are our children in immediate danger."

Raven leaned forward on her crossed knee, looking me straight in the eye. "Yes."

I nodded. "Who's after coming after them?"

Raven closed her eyes, tilting her head to the side. When she opened them, they flared a brilliant green. "It's unclear, but it's someone from your past."

My blood suddenly ran cold. "A man or a woman?"

"A man," she replied. "In fact, this man who is after your children is not after them for their powers."

"He's after revenge," I finished as chills ran over my body.

"I'm afraid so." Raven nodded. "And he will do anything to get it."

I took a long swig of my wine. "I feared that my past sins would come back to haunt me one day. But I didn't dream my children would be in danger because of it."

Leila gave my hand a gentle squeeze, gaining my attention. "We'll face this together."

Raven nodded, smiling as she took Leila in. "You look marvelous, my dear. Vampirism becomes you."

Leila nodded, smiling. "Thank you, but it was necessary."

A crease formed between Raven's eyes. "You didn't want to become a vampire?"

"Yes, of course I did." Leila bit her lower lip. "It was the only way I could protect my children and to be able to survive in this world."

Raven nodded, understanding. "Leila, let me know when you're ready to begin your witch training. You have a lot of potential."

"Thank you," Leila replied. "But I'm not sure when we'll be in New York. In the meantime, I'll speak with Annette Depraysue to see if she can start my training."

"As you wish." Raven sighed. "Just promise me that you'll think of letting the children come with me. Their experience will be what they need to succeed at uniting the species one day."

"But they're only children," I replied.

"Children with the purpose of uniting the species—"

"When they're older," Leila finished. "But we'll promise to think about it."

Raven nodded, understanding.

"The only way I'll consider it is if a bodyguard goes with them for each of the children," I said, giving Leila's hand a gentle squeeze.

"But they're just children." Leila released my hand and turned back to Raven. "But we'll promise to think about it."

"Yes, of course. But keep in mind, you can come to visit them in New York as often as you like." Raven took another sip of her wine. "If you don't mind, I'll stay the night to give you time to think about it."

"I'll go with them... when the time comes."

I looked back, and Addie was standing in the doorway of the hallway. "Where are the children?"

"In the family room. I came out to check on lunch for the children and overheard." Adeline let out a deep breath. "When they go to Mayfield Manor, I look young enough to go with them." She shrugged. "I'll pose as a student, and no one will know that I'm their protector."

I nodded. "You won't be able to be with both children at once, so Sirena will need a protector. We can start looking right away."

"As we said, we'll think about it." Leila pursed her lips. "But there's no way I can send my children off alone right now."

"They won't be alone." Raven smiled. "I have a whole coven who will become their protectors."

Just then, there was a knock on the door. I quickly crossed the room, and room service was there with our meal.

"You can set it up on the table," Leila instructed as waiters dressed in black pants and white shirts pushed in a serving cart, helping them set everything up. The whole time, she never once looked over at me.

At that moment, I knew that if I allowed our children to go with Raven, she'd never forgive me. It was something that we would definitely have to discuss before we make any decisions, and we both would have to be in agreement.

"I'll get the children." Addie started to walk away when I stopped her.

"Adeline, don't tell the children what you overheard just yet. Their mother and I have to discuss it first before any decisions are made."

She looked over at me and nodded. "Yes, of course." Then she headed down the hallway.

I got another bottle of wine for dinner and poured some for the adults, and a glass for Addie, too.

Addie came back a moment later with the children, and Leila scooped Sirena up and set her at the table. Then she kissed her cheek, along with Jase, as if she knew what was coming.

"Raven." I smiled as I held her chair, and she took her seat, then I did the same for Leila.

I kissed Leila's cheek, but she didn't even offer me a smile. Leila had waited a long time to have children, and so have I. But for the children to be taken from us so soon was heartbreaking for us both.

"Well, shall we?" I asked, taking my usual seat at the head of the table. Then I reached over and gave Leila's hand a gentle squeeze, hoping to convey that I had no intention of letting the children go any more than she.

She looked up at me, and a small smile lit her lips.

Even though Raven could read our minds and knew what we were thinking, she never let on. As we enjoyed our meal with our children and Raven, I just hoped it wasn't the last.

CHAPTER 7

Lance

"Would you like me to show you to your room?" I asked Raven. We had just finished our meal, and she still made no move to leave, which was rare. Usually, she visited long enough to give us the news she had, and then she left. But today, she was hanging out as if waiting for something.

"Is something about to happen?" I asked, keeping my voice low.

Leila's head snapped up, her eyes filled with concern. Since she became a vampire, her hearing was just as good as mine. There was no keeping anything from her anymore, not that I did before, but still....

Raven stared into my eyes and smiled. "I'll stay with Leila and the children for a while to visit, if that's alright."

"Yes, of course."

Indirectly, she had answered my question. I would be called away, and she would stay here with Leila and the children.

Raven nodded, having read my thoughts.

Just then, my cell phone rang, and I quickly looked down to check the caller ID. "It's Drake."

"Drake, what's wrong?" I quickly walked into the salon and closed the door so the children wouldn't hear.

"The East Coven is under attack!" he yelled into the phone. "I just received word from Darius Blanchard. He needs us now!"

"I'm on my way," I replied. "I'll notify the Diamond Pack, too. I'll meet you there."

"And Lance?"

"Yes?"

"Bring everyone you have to spare from your coven."

"Leila, I have to go," I said, hanging up the phone. "The East Coven is under attack."

"I'm coming, too—"

"No. Stay here with the children." I pulled her to my chest. "Remember, your priority is to protect the children." Then I crushed my lips to hers in a quick but meaningful kiss. "I'll be back as soon as I can."

"Raven?" My eyes shot up to meet hers.

"I will stay here with Leila and the children," she quickly replied.

"Go!" Leila said, already walking with me to the door. "Be safe and come back soon."

"I will." I gave her another quick kiss and closed the door behind me. "Do not let anyone enter the penthouse under any circumstances!" I ordered the guards, heading toward the stairs as I dialed Kellen's number.

"Yes, sir!" they both said in unison.

"Kellen here," he said on the first ring.

"Leave enough men here to guard the castle but get every able-bodied man you can and meet me in the courtyard. The East Coven is under attack."

"Will do." The call cut off abruptly.

I dialed Ferdinand next. "Ferdinand, the East Coven is under attack. Stay here and secure the castle."

"Yes, sir," he replied.

"And this time, if anything happens to my family while I'm gone, I will take your head when I return. Got it?"

There was a slight pause, and then he replied. "Yes, sir."

I dialed Xander next, the Alpha of the local wolf-shifters, The Diamond Pack.

"Lance, what's up?"

"I need your help," I replied, stepping into the lobby, already filled with vampires.

His voice was suddenly serious. "What do you need?"

"The East Vampire Coven is under attack," I said, looking around the lobby. "Can you meet us there?" I walked out, headed toward the courtyard, and everyone followed. Outside, vampires were coming from all over the castle to meet me there.

"We're on our way," Xander replied. Suddenly, the line went dead.

"Everyone!" I looked around, and no humans were in sight. In the distance near the castle, vampires were blocking off the area, preventing the humans from entering the courtyard. "The East Coven is under attack! Let's go!"

We ran the back way toward the east, out of sight of the humans. The last thing we needed was to attract their attention, since it was in the middle of the day and the sun was high in the sky.

When we got there, the battle was raging. Recognizing the members of the East Coven, I saw a vampire in trouble and ripped the heart out of his attacker, and he burst into flames, along with his heart, as I dropped it to the ground.

I fought my way through the crowd, and behind me, Xander and The Diamond Pack leaped into action in their wolf forms, attacking the vampire invaders. I quickly scanned the grounds of the Compound, looking for Darius. He was fighting several vampires along with his right-hand man, Mason.

I took down several more vampires, and we were winning, when a familiar voice yelled, "Stop fighting… now!"

I looked up, and my heart stopped, for Raif's arm was wrapped around Darius' throat from behind at the top of the hill.

"No!" Darius yelled, struggling against Raif's hold. "Never surrender!"

"Quiet!" Raif's muscles bulged as he held him. "Stop fighting now of I'll rip off his head!"

Mason leaped onto the platform, but Raif shoved his hand onto his chest and pulled out his heart. He burst into flames, as my heart sank. Mason had been with Darius for centuries, and Raif had just snuffed out his life in the matter of a second.

"Stop!" I yelled, holding up my hands. "Stop fighting!"

Raif chuckled when he saw me. "Well, well! If it isn't my old friend, Lance Steel!" His muscles were more prominent than they had been before, and his eyes wilder, but it was indeed Raif.

"Raif, call off your men!" I yelled across the field, knowing he could hear me. "Let Darius go!"

A broad grin spread across Raif's face. "No, I think not!" He chuckled as his lips curled into a sneer. "According to vampire law, I am now head of this coven once I take his head!"

"No!" I yelled, stopping everyone. "If you kill him, that will make us mortal enemies! Do you really want that?"

He scoffed. "After what you did, we're already mortal

enemies." Before I could say another word, he ripped off Darius's head as vampires of his coven screamed and gasped. His body immediately burst into flames along with his head as it rolled down the hill. "According to our law, I am now the head of the East Coven!" Raif drew his sword from between his shoulder blades behind his back and pointed it at everyone present. "I am now the head of the East Coven! Submit, or my men will kill you on the spot!"

"Raif, you need to leave... now! Before I take you apart piece by piece!" I started toward him, but Drake placed his hand on my arm, stopping me.

"As conqueror of his coven, it is my right!" Raif yelled, his eyes flaring a brilliant green. "The East Coven is now mine!"

"He's right," Drake said, shaking his head. "According to vampire law, it's now his coven. It's been years since we've had a coven takeover, but here it is."

"So, I'm supposed to let him get away with this? Slaughtering a whole coven?" I yelled, my eyes flaring. "You will pay for this, Raif!"

He burst out laughing as he shook his head. "No, I think 'tis you who will pay... for what you did years ago!"

"That was a long time ago, and Selestra tricked me—"

"And she tricked you into fucking her?" he sneered. "No, you will pay, Sir Lance Steel. I can promise you that!"

"Yes!" I yelled, realizing how this sounded to everyone present, but I didn't care. He had involved my family, and now he was going to pay. "Selestra had been trying to seduce me for a long time before I finally gave in. Then she tricked you into making me a vampire and making you think that she was dead!"

"You're a liar!" he yelled, pointing his sword at me. "She loved me, and you stole her!"

I laughed without humor, shaking my head. "You can keep what doesn't want to be kept."

Suddenly, Selestra walked out from behind Raif and draped her arm over his shoulder, then he turned and grabbed her hair roughly, yanking it back as he sank his mouth down onto hers, giving her a brutal kiss. Then he pulled back and wiped the corner of his lips. "As you can see, she was never yours."

"I don't want her!" I yelled back. "But she's tricking you now! She's playing you! Can't you see that?"

"The only thing I see is a man that will pay for his sins!" Raif yelled, taking a step forward. "You took away everything that I held dear. And now, I will do the same to you."

"Stay away from my family!" I yelled. "If I see you near them, I'll rip out your heart myself!"

He burst out laughing. "You can try."

I unbuttoned my shirt and threw it down onto the ground. "Then let's do this now! This is between us! Let's not involve any more innocents!"

Raif shook his head. "No, not yet. When you least expect it, I will come for you, your children, and your wife."

A deep, guttural growl erupted from deep within my chest as I stomped toward him, but Drake stopped me again, pulling me back along with Kellen.

I looked down at Drake's hand on my arm and snarled. "Remove your hand before I remove it from your arm, old friend."

Drake let me go but stood before me, blocking my path. "Not today, Lance." Then he turned toward Raif. "I am Drake Summerfield, Leader of the South Coven! I concede and recognize you as the rightful leader of the East Coven!"

His men cheered.

"But heed my words," Drake continued, "if you come near Lance, his wife, or his children, I will take you down myself."

Raif nodded, smiling as he held up his sword and let out a victorious battle cry, reminding me of when I fought by his side years ago. But then, he was a friend. And now, my darkest enemy.

"Everyone, it's over!" Drake yelled, "Raif is now the leader of the East Coven!"

"North Coven, let's go! It's over!" I yelled, calling off my men. I started to walk away when Raif stopped me.

"Sir Lance Steel!"

I turned to look at him, grinding my teeth.

"This isn't over between us!" he yelled, pointing his sword at me. "One day, I will come for you, and you will pay!"

"No!" I yelled back. "'Tis you, Sir Raif Cavanaugh, who will pay!" Then I turned and walked away with my coven.

"Drake, don't trust him." I shook my head as we walked away. "He's as strong as they come and a devil in battle, as you saw." I turned to face him. "But from here on out, do not stand in my way. If you do, then we're no longer friends."

Drake nodded once. "Lance, what good would you be to Leila

and the kids if you're dead?"

"You didn't think I could take him?" I yelled, my voice raising several octaves.

He nodded. "Yes, you could take him. But with his coven fighting with him, I didn't want to take the chance on one of them interfering. If it came down to a fair fight to the death between you and Raif, I'd stand back and let you go for it. But with his men surrounding him, it's a different story."

"But my men—"

"Will fight to the death for you," Drake cut me off. "But do you really want to lose any more of your them?" Drake stepped in front of me, looking into my eyes. "I promise, there will be a time and a place. But now isn't it. Trust me on that."

I nodded once, knowing he was right. "But mark my words. If he steps one foot on my castle grounds, he's a dead man."

Drake nodded. "Agreed."

I ran with my men back to my coven as quickly as possible, hoping Raif hadn't planned on launching an attack on my castle while I wasn't there. As soon as I got there, Ferdinand handed me a shirt when I walked past and followed me.

"Has there been an attack while I was gone?" I headed up the stairs instead of taking the elevator, needing to see my family and ensure their safety.

"No, it's been quiet," Ferdinand said behind me.

Upstairs, there were two guards by the door, along with Raven's bodyguards, and two more strolling the halls, keeping a close eye on the penthouse. Obviously, Ferdinand took me seriously this time.

"More guards?"

He nodded. "I didn't want the same thing that happened last time to happen again."

"Good man." I nodded as I walked past the guards and into the penthouse.

"Oh, Lance!" Leila quickly crossed the room to me and pulled me in for a hug. "Are you okay?"

I nodded, looking around the penthouse. "I'm fine. Where are the children?"

"Addie has them in the family room," she replied.

Raven stood and folded her hands. "Well, now that you're safe, I'll go to the guest condo to give you two time to discuss. Would you mind if I stayed the night? I'll leave tomorrow."

"Raven, you're welcome here anytime." I crossed the room to her and gently squeezed her hands as I looked into her eyes. "Thank you for the warning and for your inquiry. Leila and I will discuss your proposition and will let you know before you leave."

Raven nodded and then placed her hand on my cheek. "I'm so sorry about your friend."

It still amazed me that even though I hadn't told her, she already knew. It made me wonder what else she might know that she hadn't shared. But on second thought, I didn't want to know.

"Raven, I'll show you to your room." I looked over at Leila. "I'll be right back."

Leila nodded as she pulled Raven in for a hug. "Thanks for staying with me during the crisis." She let out a deep breath, a crease forming between her eyes. "Just so you know, I understand why you came. We also appreciate your offer and your willingness to protect our children."

Raven reached out and squeezed her arm. "You and Lance are not in this alone. We'll get through this together."

Leila nodded, giving her a small smile. "We truly appreciate that."

"But just to let you know, I would never try to interfere with you raising your children." Then Raven leaned in conspiratorially, lowering her voice. "And I would never try to take your place... or Lance's."

"I know that." Leila pulled her in for another hug. But when she released her, there were tears in her eyes.

I pulled Leila in for a hug, too, and kissed her forehead. "I'll be right back."

I draped Raven's cloak around her shoulders and offered her my arm. Then I led her into the hallway and made a left at the end into another hallway as her guards followed.

"Lance, I know my offer is difficult for you and Leila to consider, and I know it comes at a bad time, but I wouldn't be here if it wasn't necessary." She gave me a sympathetic look.

I nodded, letting out a sigh. "I know that, and we truly appreciate it."

"Just please tell me you'll consider it—"

"I will, but it's something that Leila and I will have to discuss."

She let out a deep breath as a smile lit her lips. "I completely understand. Take your time." Then she kissed my cheek. "I'll see you and Leila in the morning."

I opened the door for her, and she disappeared inside as her guards stood outside her door, leaving me to wonder what would happen if we refused.

CHAPTER 8

Leila

After cleaning up the penthouse and putting everything away, I headed down the hallway toward the family room. The children were playing Chess with Addie again.

"Is everything okay?" I asked, sitting on the small sofa along the wall.

It was already time to think about remodeling again. Sirena was too big for the rocking horse now, and Jase had outgrown it a while back. They were growing up too fast. And if they went away with Raven, I was sure to miss the rest of their short childhood, too.

"Mom, what's wrong?" Sirena sat beside me and held my hand.

I pulled her onto my lap and held her close. "Nothing, baby doll. Mommy's just thinking."

"What about?" she asked, too bright for her young years.

I smiled, kissing her cheek. "Nothing, baby. Everything's fine." I gave her another hug and then set her down. "Why don't you play Chess with Addie and Jase while I talk to Daddy?"

She nodded, a crease forming between her eyes. "Okay, Mom." Then she hurried over and slid onto Jase's lap. He looked up at me and frowned, then turned his attention back to their game.

What would he think about us sending him and his sister off to live with Raven? Even though it would be for training and to keep them safe, try explaining that to a child who needs his mother.

And what of Sirena? She was already growing too quickly, and I've had such a short time with her. I fear her anger may turn her into an evil witch... literally. And that's the last thing I'd ever want.

I looked up, and Lance was standing in the doorway, leaning on the wall, watching the children, as concerned as I was.

I stood beside him and slid my arm around his waist, and he

wrapped his arm around my shoulder as we watched the children. Obviously, he was thinking the same thing I was. It wasn't an easy decision to make with no easy answers.

I kissed his cheek and headed down the hallway as he followed. We had a lot to discuss, and neither of us wanted to have this conversation.

"Want some blood?" I took out two blood bags just in case and put them in the microwave.

He nodded, sliding his arms around me as he leaned his head on my shoulder. "Please."

I slid my arms over his, enjoying the feeling of safety in his arms. But in our world, safety was an illusion.

He let me go and leaned against the counter, watching me.

I cut open the blood bags, poured them into long-stemmed glasses, and handed one to Lance, knowing what he was going to say. I took a sip, letting the crimson liquid work its magic throughout my body. For this conversation, I would need all the strength I could get.

"So, you think we should let the children go with Raven."

He pursed his lips as he set his glass down on the counter and rubbed my arms. "You must understand what happened today."

"Raif?"

Lance nodded. "And Selestra."

He took a deep breath as he picked up his glass and took me by the hand. Then he led me into our bedroom and closed the door behind us. But instead of sitting on the bed, he led me to the club chairs and table in front of the window. Then he held my chair for me and across from me.

"Leila, I have to tell you what happened today, and I didn't want the children to overhear."

I nodded and took another sip. "I'm ready."

"Raif killed Darius Blanchard today."

I gasped, my eyes wide. "Darius? Why?"

Lance sighed. "He took over his coven. Leila, he has an army with him, and they overpowered the East Coven and slaughtered Darius and Mason right before everyone."

"Oh, my God!"

He nodded. "And according to our laws, he is now the head of the East Coven."

"But how?" I scoffed, shaking my head. "He should be brought before the Tribunal for judgment for leading an unprovoked attack!"

Lance shook his head. "It's an old law, but valid. According to Vampire Law, he who kills the head of a coven becomes the head. There hasn't been a takeover like that in a very long time, but I witnessed it today."

I nodded, understanding. "So, he now has a coven here in Las Vegas."

Lance sighed. "And he's vowed to make my life hell. He pointed me out and told me that he will not rest until I lose everything I hold dear."

"Me and the children." I took another sip of the blood. "So, we stand and fight!"

"Leila...." He took my hand in his as he looked into my eyes. "I want you and the children to go to New York with Raven—"

"No! Absolutely not!" I bolted from my chair and started pacing. "If you think for one moment that I'd leave you alone to fight when an attack is coming, then think again."

Lance let out a deep breath and smiled as he raised my hand to his lips and kissed it. "Leila, you know I love you, but if you go with the children to New York, you'll be able to keep them safe—"

"I'm not leaving you." Tears filled my eyes. "Raven can protect the children, I have no doubt, and we can visit them on the weekends. There's nonstop flights to New York, or we can take the Learjet." Lance bought a new one as soon as things settled down after the explosion that took the other, and this one was new and improved. "We can leave on Friday, spend the weekend with the children, and then come back Sunday night."

He nodded, understanding. "Leila, I don't want the children to go alone—"

"Neither do I!" I shook my head. "But we're stronger together. And Raven has sworn that her whole coven will protect the children." I let out a deep breath. "Addie said she would go to New York to be Jase's protector, but Sirena needs one." Then it dawned on me as I looked into his eyes. "Kellen. He would do it. I trust him beyond all measure, and he would protect our daughter."

Lance nodded. "I was thinking of him, too. And when she goes to high school or college, he looks young enough to blend in, even though he was turned when he was twenty-five."

I nodded as tears welled up in my eyes. "I was wracking my brain, trying to think of someone on this short notice, but he was the only one I'd trust explicitly. On the other hand, we thought we could trust Jeremy, too, and he ended up betraying us. So, we had to be careful who we send with the children."

Lance nodded, looking down at my hand as he ran his fingers over mine. "I know you don't want the children to go, and neither do I. But with Raif coming after them, I'd never forgive myself if something happens to the children... or you."

I nodded. "I know, but I'm staying here with you. I don't want to send the children away at all. But I'm not leaving without you. The only way I'd go is to help settle the children in, but you need to come with us, too."

He shook his head, his eyes misty. "I can't leave the coven, not when an attack is imminent."

"I understand." Tears slid slowly down my cheeks, and then I stood and turned toward the window, wrapping my arms around myself.

"Hey...." Lance pulled me into his arms and to his chest. "It's not like we'll never see them again." He moved my hair over my shoulder and kissed my neck.

I nodded, sobbing. "I know, but it doesn't make it any easier."

"Shush...." He swept me into his arms and sat on the bed as he set me on his lap and cradled me to his chest. "Leila, I have a house in New York… a mansion. We can stay there when we visit. I'll contact the staff and tell them we're coming."

I nodded. "You mean, I'll be going. Lance, the children... it'll never be the same again after they've gone."

"I know...." He laid on the bed and held me close, cradling me. "But we can see them any time we like. In fact, you can stay there for a while to settle the children in—"

"No." I shook my head, unable to stop the tears cascading down my cheeks. "I'll only go up there for a weekend at a time, unless you come with me. I won't stay away from you for any length of time—"

"Leila, please—"

"If you ask me to do that, then you may as well ask me for a divorce." I sat up, wiping my hand across my cheeks.

"A divorce?" Lance scoffed. "Where did that come from?"

"I won't do the long-distance relationship thing with you, Lance." I stood and looked out the window to collect my thoughts. Then I turned back to face him. "So, don't ask me to. Not unless you want a divorce.”

“Never.” He quickly crossed the room to me, but I wouldn’t be consoled. “Leila, for vampires, a week, a month, even a year is nothing.”

“It is to me.” I squared my shoulders. “I’m still a new vampire, so I judge time by the ways of humans. So, please don’t ask me to leave you unless you want a divorce. I won’t leave you for any length of time. If you ever cheated on me—”

“Hey, hey....” Lance rubbed my arms as he looked into my eyes. “You are it for me! There will never be anyone else but you for me. I don’t care if we’re apart for a hundred years; I’ll never cheat on you.” Then he pulled me to his chest. “But if you ever cheated on me because I wasn’t with you, I’d never forgive myself.”

“I’d never cheat on you, Lance. But I can tell you that I’d die of a broken heart without you.” Tears spilled down my cheeks again. “Even if vampires can’t die that way, I would.”

He swept me into his arms and carried me to the bed. Then his lips crushed down onto mine as passion overtook us both.

My heart pounded as his lips groped mine. I slid my hands under his shirt and then tore it away. He threw the shredded pieces onto the floor and slid my dress up over my head, and cast it away, too.

Then I unbuckled his pants and wrapped my hand around his length, as he let out a deep moan. I pulled his lips to mine, and he ripped off my underwear and bra and pushed into me hard, taking me all at once as I gasped.

“Did I hurt you?” His eyes searched mine as he paused.

“No, never.” Gripping his back, I pulled him to me, raising my hips to meet his as he thrust into me over and again.

“I love you, Lance.” I pushed against him, and he took me deep, rolling his hips into mine.

“I love you, too,” he breathed against my skin, pushing deeply into me. “Always.”

He thrust his hips into me as he pulled back to look into my eyes, truly making love to me.

My heart pounded as he took me until my walls clenched around him, and I moaned in release. Lance covered my mouth, swallowing my moans as his length swelled and his cum shot into me, filling me with warmth and love.

Then I turned him over and straddled him, for once was never enough. I slammed onto him, running my fingers down his chest, pushing harder and faster as he massaged my breasts and fingered my nipples. Until finally, we fell over the edge together.

Then he pulled me to him, cradling me in his arms, both of us nude as he pushed my hair back away from my face. He kissed my neck and pulled back to look into my eyes. "How you can think for one moment that I could ever make love to another woman is beyond my comprehension. There is, and never will be, anyone else but you for me."

I nodded, understanding as I held him close. "Lance, I feel the same way." After a long moment, I sat up on the bed and shook my head. "Lance, I feel like we're losing our family."

"Hey...." He ran his fingers through my hair and held my neck, forcing me to look into his eyes. "We'll never lose our family. Never."

But as he held me in his arms, I couldn't help but wonder if it was true.

We spent the rest of the evening with the children, laughing and playing games as a family, not knowing when we'd see each other again.

CHAPTER 9

Lance

Bang, bang, bang!

"Stay here." I jumped out of bed the next morning, slipped on my trousers, and grabbed a shirt. "I'll be right back."

Leila nodded, already out of bed and slipping into her robe. "Who could it be this early?"

"I don't know, but hurry and get dressed." I hurried to the door, and Raven was standing on the other side when I opened it. "Raven, is everything okay?"

She shook her head. "No, it isn't. May I come in?"

"Yes, of course." I stepped back to let her in.

She wrung her hands, pacing. "I have to take the children... now."

"What?" I asked, buttoning my dress shirt. "I thought you weren't going to leave until this afternoon."

"I wasn't," she replied. "But I have to take them now." She grabbed my shoulders, looking into my eyes. "Trust me on this."

"With my life," I replied. "What is it?"

"Someone's coming for the children. They're on their way."

"Who?"

I looked up, and Leila was standing in the doorway of the bedroom, shell shocked.

"I'm not sure, but it's someone from your past," Raven replied. "We must hurry."

"Leila, get the children ready." I pulled out my cell phone as she hurried past.

We had already packed the children's things the night before and had talked to them. It wouldn't take much to send them with Raven now.

I quickly dialed Ferdinand's number.

"Hello, Lance."

My blood ran cold. For Ferdinand's wasn't the voice I heard. It was Raif. "Where's Ferdinand?"

"That's not the question you should ask."

"Lance, the children are gone!" Leila screamed as she ran out of the back room.

"Where are they?" I gripped the phone so tightly that I nearly crushed it. "If you harm a hair on their head, you're a dead man!"

Raif scoffed. "So, Lance Steel, how does it feel to have the people you love ripped out of your life?"

"I'll kill you!" I screamed when suddenly, the line went dead. I flung open the front door, and ash fell onto the door. A pile of ash lay just outside the door, and other piles lay in the form of bodies nearby. It was evident that they died trying to keep them out. But I wondered why I hadn't heard them. Raven's bodyguards were there. One was standing and the other, on one knee, next to the other body.

"Lance, one was propped against your door, and the other is here."

I nodded as I hit Kellen's number on speed dial.

"Lance? What's wrong?" he answered on the first ring.

"The children are gone, Ferdinand's missing, and my guards are dead!"

"I'll lock down the castle right away," Kellen replied. "And Lance? Don't worry. We'll find your children."

I closed the door behind me so Leila couldn't hear. "What if he already killed them?"

"No, he wouldn't. He's probably holding them but won't kill them until you're there to watch."

"Which means we still have time." I nodded, even though he couldn't see. "Gather as many men as you can and meet me downstairs."

"You got it." Kellen paused, his footsteps picking up in the distance. Suddenly, Leila burst through the door dressed in a black leather coat, boots, and a white T-shirt, and black leather pants, prepared to fight. "Do you think he has them at the East Coven?"

"I'm not sure, but it's the best place to start."

"Agreed."

As soon as I cut off the call, I turned to Leila. "You're not going!"

"Oh, yes, I am!" Leila stared into my eyes. "Lance, they're my children, too! I'm going!"

I stared at her for a long moment and nodded. "Let's go but do everything I tell you."

"Yes, sir." She stared at me, her eyes determined, and walked with a strong gait.

"Stay with your master!" I yelled at Raven's bodyguards. "Do not let anyone in!"

"Aye!" they both yelled in unison.

Leila and I took the stairs two at a time. In the lobby, the castle was locked down, and the casino had been evacuated.

"I want every inch of this castle searched for Raif and Selestra!" I growled to Kellen. "They have my children!"

"Also, Addie's missing." Leila bit her lower lip. "You don't think she had anything to do with this. Do you?"

"No," Kellen quickly replied. "She loves those kids. There's no way that she was behind this."

I nodded. "Well, we shall soon see."

"If they got past Addie, there was many of them." Kellen looked over at Javier. "Search the castle! Now!"

"Also, Ferdinand is missing," I added. "Raif had his phone."

"Well, if that's the case, then he's dead." Kellen shook his head. "After the last time, there's no way he would let anyone take the children without a fight."

Javier and Channing came back a moment later. "The castle's secure."

"Obviously not very secure, if Raif could come for my children while we were sleeping!" I growled. "Javier, keep the castle secure and post guards. Close down the casino, and don't let anyone in or out until we return."

Kellen shot a look over to my wife. "Leila, you really shouldn't—"

"I'm going," she said flatly. "Either with you or alone."

"Let's go!" I yelled and headed out the door. "Leila, stay with me."

"Aye!"

She ran beside me, keeping up the whole way. We ran through the desert and over mountains, the sun high in the sky, beating down on us. But extreme heat and cold didn't affect vampires. Soon, the Compound of the East Coven came into view.

"Let me do the talking," I said to everyone present.

"Halt right there, Mr. Steel!" the guard yelled while we were still a distance away. "I have orders not to let you in!"

"Damn your orders!" I shouted, quickly approaching. "Either let me in, or I'll go in by force! He has my children!"

The guard snarled, staring at me for a moment, then he nodded. "Let them through!" Then he placed a hand on my chest, stopping me. "But if there's any violence while you're here, I'm holding you personally responsible."

"Remove your hand from my chest, sir, before I rip it off." My eyes flared, staring into his eyes.

He lowered his hand and let me pass.

I stormed through the Compound until I came to the throne room, where Darius used to pass judgment on members of his coven. Raif was sitting there with Selestra draped all over him.

"Where are my children?" I growled, clenching my fists.

Selestra's head snapped up.

"So, Lance…." A broad smile spread across Raif's face. "How does it feel to have what you hold most dear taken from you?"

"Give me back my children!" Leila screamed, starting toward him, but I stopped her.

"Well!" Raif chuckled. "I see you brought the little missus this time! I think I just might kill her, too."

"Over my dead body," I stormed toward him, but Raif was already on his feet.

"If you kill me, you'll never find your children!" Raif growled as Selestra took a step back. "You took everything from me!"

I scoffed, inclining my head toward Selestra. "Obviously, I haven't taken everything."

"She came back to me after you left her, alone and defenseless!" He walked purposefully toward me.

I burst out laughing. "There is no way that bitch is defenseless! So, she turned you, huh?"

"She turned me before she ever left with you," he growled. "How do you think I survived all those battles in the Crusades?"

I scoffed, nodding. "So, all this time, you were already a vampire? She didn't fake her death, after all. You knew she was still alive. But you thought you had killed me. You didn't know she had given me her blood." After all these years, it all suddenly made sense.

"Of course, I killed you! You were my friend, and I caught you fucking my wife! You betrayed me, Lance!" Raif growled.

"Selestra kept coming on to me, and I ignored her advances," I replied. "And then she orchestrated the ruse about her mother, and you asked me to escort her because you were called by the king! As a friend, I agreed to escort her, and I resisted her advances... until I could resist no longer." I waved my hand in her direction. "I accept responsibility for what I did, but she seduced me, your best friend, and you forgave her! Why can you not do the same for me?"

He laughed without humor. "You think you can apologize, and all will be well?" One corner of his lip raised into a snarl. "After what you did?"

"I apologize for betraying you," I said, meaning every word. "I can't tell you how many times I wished I could tell you, but I thought you were long gone." I bit my lower lip and released it. "Raif, you were my best friend, and I miss you. I miss our friendship."

He scoffed. "You miss our friendship." He took a step forward, glaring at me. "Do you think I could ever forgive you... after what you've done? I trusted you, and you betrayed me!"

"End this nonsense now and give me back my children! They are innocents!" I stepped closer to him, looking him straight in the eye. "And as knights, we do not harm the innocent. We live by a code, Raif! Or have you forgotten?"

"Oh, I remember. But you, Sir Lance, are the one who abandoned the code when you fucked my woman!" He looked over my shoulder at Leila and licked his bottom lip. "And I look forward to returning the favor."

"Give me back my children!" Leila growled.

Selestra looked between us, her eyes wide. If I didn't know any better, I would have thought that she didn't know he had my children. But that was just like her, never claiming responsibility for anything she did.

Raif laughed. "I think I'll keep your children and raise them as my own." He took another step closer. "And I will turn them against you."

"Mark my words," I growled, stepping closer. "Once I have my children back, I will have your head." Then my head snapped up toward Selestra. "Selestra, where are my children?"

"I... I... I don't know." And from the look in her eyes, she really didn't.

"Liar!" Leila screamed. "You were in on it with him! You took my children while we slept!"

"I didn't—" Selestra said, confused.

"Stop!" Raif growled at her. "Selestra, stay quiet, or I'll rip your heart out myself!"

Fear ran through her eyes... and she had never been afraid of anything.

"What have you done to her?" I growled, nodding toward Selestra.

He scoffed as he stepped closer, nose to nose. "I... made... her... pay."

My fist flew into his face, sending him flying backward. Then I jumped on him, wrapping my fists around his throat and pounded his head against the cold, stone floor. "Where are my children?"

"Let him go!" Selestra yelled. My head snapped up, and her arm was around Leila's throat from behind.

"Let me go!" Leila clawed at her arm, her fingernails leaving bloody streaks, but Selestra didn't even flinch.

My heart sank as I held Raif by the throat. "I'll let him go when you let her go."

"Done." She released her, and I released Raif.

Raif punched me in the face, but I just turned my head, staring into his eyes.

"Leila, let's go." Bringing Leila was a mistake. If I tore Raif apart right now, I'd never find the children. But in the meantime, Selestra could kill Leila in an instant. No, the best thing to do was to take Leila out of here and come back alone. Then I stared into Raif's eyes. "Once I find my children and my family is safe, I will rip your heart out and watch as you burn."

"I'm not leaving without my children!" Leila screamed, wrenching my heart as I grabbed her around the waist, pulling her back. "Let me go, Lance! I'm not leaving without them!"

"Leila, we'll get them back," I whispered. "I promise."

"Liar!" she screamed as I pulled her away. "I want my children!"

I threw Leila over my shoulder and turned to face Raif. "Mark my words. If anything happens to my children, I will not stop until it rains blood."

A demonic laugh resonated from Raif, but he made no effort to stop us from leaving.

Selestra looked on, a crease forming between her eyes.

"Leila, I've never lied to you before," I cooed as I carried her out of the Compound. "Why would I lie now?"

I pulled her to me, and she beat her fists against my chest as tears rushed down her cheeks. "I want my children!" Then she collapsed into my arms as she sobbed, ripping my heart out.

"Shush...." I stroked her hair, pushing it away from her face. "I'll come back, and I'll find them. But I can't risk losing you, too."

She shook her head, wiping her hand over her cheeks. "You were right. I shouldn't have come. Lance, I'm so sorry—"

"Shush, love," I cooed, knowing we had to go... now. "I know you didn't mean it. Now, let's go before Raif changes his mind about letting us leave." I grabbed her face, forcing her to look into my eyes. "We have to go."

"Not without my children."

In one fluid motion, I flipped her over my shoulder and nodded toward Kellen and the others for them to follow. I ran with her out of the Compound as I made a silent vow. Raif was going to pay.

CHAPTER 10

Leila

"Put me down!" I yelled when we arrived back at our castle. "I'm in control now."

Lance set me on my feet as he looked into my eyes, ripping out my heart. "Leila, I promise you, we'll get the children back."

I nodded. "I know. Lance, I'm so sorry I called you a liar. I was just—"

"I know." He pulled me to his chest as I held him, gripping his shirt.

"Lance, I—" Then it hit me as I looked into his eyes. "Raven's still here."

"I know, but—"

"No, Lance!" I cut him off. "Maybe she can help us find the children."

He let out a deep breath. "You're right." He motioned with his head toward the stairs. "Let's go!"

We darted up the stairs and were on the top floor within seconds. Down the hall, two guards stood outside our door along with Raven's guards.

"Has anyone entered or exited the penthouse while we were away?" Lance demanded.

Javier shook his head. "No, sir."

"Thank you." Lance opened the door and stood back, letting me go in first.

"Raven," I said, quickly crossing the room to her. "Do you know a spell that can help us locate our children?"

"Yes, of course." She rose from her seat. "I can do a locator spell. But Leila, I'll need your magic, too."

My eyes widened. "*My* magic? But I haven't been trained—"

"You don't have to be." She headed over to the table as we followed.

I nodded. "What can we do?"

"Both of you stand on either side of the table."

Lance and I quickly did as she said.

"Do you know where the children are?" I asked, knowing she knew something that she wasn't telling us.

She shook her head. "No, but I can tell you that someone is with them, keeping them safe."

My head snapped up to Lance. "Addie."

He quickly nodded.

"They will be fine until we get there, but we have to hurry," she continued. "The locator spell will show us where they are, but I can't do the spell alone. Leila, you're more powerful than you think, and I need your magic."

"What can I do?" Lance asked, concern filling his eyes.

"Trust me and do as I say," Raven instructed, holding our hands. "No matter what you see, do not let go. This is the only way."

Suddenly, my blood went cold. If Raven said this was the only way, then I would do what I had to, trusting her with my life... and the lives of our children. "What now?"

When we were in place, she waved her arms over the table, and what looked to be an ancient map of the world appeared, along with a heart-shaped planchette, resembling the pointer of a Ouija board. "Now, lightly place your fingertips on the planchette and do not remove them. No matter what happens. No matter what you see."

After we did as she said, Raven chanted, *"Pueri nobis sunt monstra."*

Suddenly, power rushed from me, and the whole map lit up and glowed. Light shot up, filling the room, and then suddenly, a vision of the children came into view under our hands, deep within the table. Even though I could feel the planchette solid under my fingertips, I could see nothing but a three-dimensional movie of the children. Then I realized it was live.

"Jase! Sirena!" I yelled.

Jase was holding his sister, but his head snapped up, hearing my voice.

"If you can hear me, we're coming for you!" I yelled.

Jase nodded once as he held his sister, protecting her as Lance had told him.

"Don't let go! No matter what you see!" Raven yelled. *"Ostende nobis ubi siti sunt filii!"*

Suddenly, we were pulled back away from the vision, and the world map became visible again. Then it zoomed in deeper, going farther into the map until the aerial view of a warehouse came into view.

"I know where that is." Lance let out a deep breath. "It's a warehouse on the edge of the Oasis."

Raven nodded. As soon as she lifted her hands from the planchette, the image disappeared, and the ancient world map was left in its place. She waved her hand, and it disappeared.

"Let's go," I said, already headed toward the door.

"No!" Lance yelled, pulling me back.

"Lance." Raven placed her hand on his shoulder. "We're all going."

Lance stared at her for a moment, clenching his jaw. "Then let's go." His head snapped up and he looked into my eyes. "Stay with me and do exactly as I say."

I nodded once, knowing I would do anything to get the children back.

Raven nodded, and we headed toward the door. "Lance, bring as many men as you can, and I'll do the same. Have them meet us at the warehouse."

A crease formed between his eyes, but he nodded. Then he pulled out his cell phone and quickly dialed it. He started talking in clipped tones to Kellen and then hung up. "They'll meet us there."

Raven nodded as we walked into the hallway. "Come." She reached out to the men, and they held her hands without further explanation.

Lance pointed toward the two guards in front of the penthouse. "Do not let anyone in or out!"

"Yes, sir!" they said in unison.

"Will we have enough men to get them back?" I asked, staring into her eyes.

Raven nodded once. Then she stood in the center of the hallway, holding each guard's hands. "Lance, Leila, hold our hands and create a circle." We did as she said. "Hold on and do not let go! We'll be traveling through the Space-Time Continuum."

I had no idea what that was, but I nodded. Then again, there was still a lot about our world that I didn't know.

"Ad filios nos transfer!"

Suddenly, we were traveling through a transparent tunnel, as dark matter and stars rushed past, the sound deafening as we zoomed through, moving without being moved, until we came to a stop in front of the children.

"Seize them!" guards yelled as soon as they saw us.

"Mommy!" Sirena yelled, running toward me.

Addie stood in front of us, donning her fighting stance. "Stay behind me!"

But I grabbed Sirena and Jase and pulled them behind me. "Stay behind me and don't look!"

Lance leaped at one guard and quickly ripped off his head as his body burst into flames. One of Raven's guards ripped out the heart of another vampire, and orange, red, and yellow flames shot up from his corpse as he fell to the ground, along with his heart. Raven's other guard ripped the head off the last vampire, holding it by the hair, and then dropped it onto the floor as it burst into flames, along with the body. Addie didn't move from in front of us, standing as protector over the children and me the whole time.

"Where's Selestra and Raif?" I yelled, holding the children behind me.

"They were here earlier, but they left," Addie replied.

"Leila, stay here with the children!" Lance and Addie darted quickly out the door, but Raven's guards stayed with her. Lance and Addie came back a moment later.

Lance sighed. "They're nowhere to be found. Let's get the children out of here. We can find them later."

"Everyone, hold hands and don't let go." Raven pushed her long black hair back over her shoulders and held her guard's hands. Lance and I held the children's hands, and then Lance nodded to Raven. *"Transporte nos ad penthouse* Caprice Casino!"

Again, wind rushed past as we traveled through the Space-Time Continuum, through the transparent tunnel as dark matter and stars zoomed past. We came to a stop a moment later inside the penthouse.

"Oh, my God! Jase! Sirena! Are you okay?" I grabbed Sirena up and pulled Jase to me, hugging them both.

"Oh, my God!" Lance wrapped his arms around us as we both hugged them. Then he looked up at Raven, sincerity prevalent in his eyes. "Raven, how can we ever repay you? Thank you so much!"

Raven stared at him, sadness filling her eyes... and I knew. For their own safety, we had to let the children go with Raven.

I looked up at Lance, tears threatening to spill over, his eyes heavy, too.

"Leila," he said, stepping close. "It's the only way."

I nodded as tears spilled down my cheeks. Then I stooped down and pulled the children close. "Jase, Sirena, for your own safety, you'll need to stay with Aunt Raven for a while as we talked about last night. But Dad and I will come and visit you every weekend and as often as possible. You need training, and she'll keep you safe."

Jase rubbed my shoulder, looking into my eyes. "It's okay, Mom. I'm ready. And I'll take care of Sirena while we're away, too."

"Thank you, son," I said, pulling him in for a hug. "How did you get to be so grown up?"

Jase smiled as sadness filled his eyes.

Then Lance hugged him, too. "Jase, as I said, you're one of the men of this house. And as such, it's up to us to protect the women."

Jase nodded, smiling. "I know, Dad. I'll protect her like I did when Selestra and Raif had us."

Lance grabbed him up off his feet and hugged him tightly. "I love you, son."

"I love you, too, Dad," he replied.

I kissed Sirena and Jase's foreheads. "Sirena, you look out for your brother, too. Okay?"

She nodded frantically. If I didn't know any better, I would have thought that she had grown in the day they were gone. "Don't worry, Mom! I'll take care of him!"

Everyone laughed.

"Leila," Raven said, stepping close. "You should come with us and train, too."

But I quickly shook my head. "I'll have Annette train me here. I can go to her coven for training, but I'll be close."

"Hey, Mom and Dad!" Jase said, clearly excited. "Once Mom learns the transportation spell, you can come visit us any time!"

I nodded, smiling through my tears. "I promise to learn it soon."

Raven stepped up beside us. "It's time."

I pulled her in for a hug, too, as she patted my back. "Take good care of my children, Raven," I said when I pulled back.

She nodded as she placed her hand on my cheek. "I will. I promise."

Addie stepped forward. "With your permission, I'd like to go as their protector."

Lance nodded. "By all means." Then he glanced over at Raven. "Would you mind?"

She shook her head, smiling. "No. Not at all. She can train with us."

My head snapped up. "Does Addie have magic, too?"

A smile lit Raven's face. "Addie, would you like to tell them, or should I?"

"I'm a hybrid, too, half witch and half vampire. But like you, Leila, I never developed my powers." Then Addie looked over at Raven and chuckled. "This should be interesting."

Raven nodded, returning her smile. "This is your journey, too." Then she turned to Lance. "Sirena will need a protector eventually, too. But for now, I'll assign her one from my coven. But when she comes home, she'll need one."

Lance nodded. "We've already worked it out. Kellen said he would serve as her protector when it's time."

A broad smile spread across Raven's face. "A perfect choice."

"Raven, we'll bring their clothes and personal belongings when we come," I said, trying to hold back the tears.

"Don't worry. I'll see that they have what they need until then, but we must leave now."

I nodded. "I understand." Then I looked into the children's eyes. "You both are our life. Daddy and I both love you very much."

Lance placed his hand on my shoulder, and I took a step back, knowing it was time.

Raven and her guards held the children's hands and then she yelled, *"Transporte nos in strumam meam Novi Eboraci!"*

Suddenly, white, gold, and silver sparkles zoomed in and swirled around them in a tornado of sparks as wind rushed in. A moment later, they were gone.

Silence.

It was suddenly much too quiet.

Then I turned and collapsed in Lance's arms as we cried together, not knowing when we'd see our children again.

CHAPTER 11

Lance

Four Months Later

"Good morning, love," I said, greeting Leila one morning. She looked as sexy as ever after stepping out of the shower.

"Morning," she replied, sadness in her eyes. "I'll be right out." Then she walked into the dressing room and locked it behind her, pain ripping through my chest.

She blamed me for the children leaving with Raven, or at least I thought she did, although she never said so.

Since the children went with Raven, Leila spent most of her time training with Annette Depraysue at the Tenebris Witch Coven. Luckily, it was close by, so Leila came home at night, but she was becoming more and more quiet, withdrawing within herself.

And I blamed myself.

If I could have protected my children better while they were here, maybe we wouldn't have had to send them away.

We receive frequent reports about the children from Raven along with pictures... and they're growing fast. Too fast. We also visit them as often as possible, but it's not the same.

Although we've looked high and low for Raif and Selestra, we haven't found them. And the children aren't safe until we catch them.

I feel as if I'm losing my family, and Raif and Selestra are to blame. If I ever see Raif again, I'll rip his heart out and watch as he burns.

Leila walked out a few minutes later, her smile gone. I rarely saw it these days.

"I made some coffee for you and a glass of blood." I smiled, holding out her chair for her. "I made French toast, too."

"Thanks." She gave me a small smile as she sat and stirred her coffee. "So, what are you going to be doing today?"

I let out a deep breath as I set a plate of French toast in front of her along with the syrup. Then I sat kitty-corner from her with a plate for myself.

"I'm going to the hospital to meet with Drake today." I arched an eyebrow. "Would you like to come with me? Maybe you could spend some time with Amy in her lab."

Leila shook her head. "No, she's been busy with the clinic."

Amy and Elias were now in charge of the clinic overseeing vampire transformations. When undergoing the process of becoming human again, the subjects become wild and sometimes out of control. So, it was necessary to quarantine them.

The transformation isn't easy, as I discovered myself when I was going through it. But thank goodness, I didn't go through with it. I found out the hard way that only vampires and supernatural creatures could survive in our world, and there was no escaping it.

"So, are you going to go to the coven to practice again?" I asked, taking a sip of my coffee.

She took a deep breath, exhausted even though vampires don't tire easily. But these last few months had taken their toll on her.

"Leila, talk to me." I let out a deep breath.

"I do talk to you." She looked down at her plate, tears filling her eyes.

"Leila, I know you blame me for the children—"

Her head snapped up. "Lance, I don't blame you at all."

"Stop saying that!" I yelled, pushing back from the table abruptly. "You haven't said two words to me since the children left!"

"Lance, I talk to you...." She looked down, and tears streamed down her cheeks. "I just miss them."

I knelt beside her and hugged her, feeling her pain because it was also mine. "I know, love, but we'll see them soon." Then I pulled back, looking into her eyes. "Hey... why don't we go see them this weekend?"

She nodded, smiling. "Yes. It's been a while."

"I know," I kissed the top of her head. "Leila, if you want, I'll bring the children back home—"

"No," she cut me off. "They're where they need to be. I'm sure of it. But it doesn't make it any easier."

I nodded, smiling as I pulled her into my arms. "Come to the hospital with me today. Let's go to lunch after we leave or do something fun." Then my lips curled into a devilish grin as I arched an eyebrow. "Shopping, maybe?"

She chuckled. "Just don't tell Angela. She'd be disappointed that we bought clothes that she didn't design."

"So, it's settled then." I smiled as I took my seat and cut into my French toast, feeling better than I had in a long time. This was the most enthusiasm Leila had shown since the children left, so maybe there was still hope after all. "We'll go to the hospital, and then we'll go out and make a day of it."

Leila smiled, nodding she took a bite of her pancake.

When we finished eating, I left the dishes in the sink for the maid. Then I took my car keys from the bowl by the door as we walked out to the elevator.

"We're not taking the limo today?" Leila smiled as she nodded toward the key in my hand.

"It's been a while since we've taken out the Lykan Hypersport, and it's time."

Leila and I needed to find a way to get the spark back in our marriage. She rarely spoke to me anymore, and she cried every night. Oftentimes, she just sat in a chair and stared off into space, missing the children. I was glad that she at least had her witch training to keep her occupied, but I was worried about her. I stepped into the elevator with her, placing my hand on the small of her back.

When the doors closed, I realized that she was not the only one to blame. Both of us felt the separation from our children, and it was taking its toll on us... on our marriage.

The doors opened, and we headed into my private garage, where all my cars were kept.

I pulled out of the garage in my Hypersport a few minutes later. I gave her hand a gentle squeeze, holding it on the way to the hospital.

"So, have you had any luck finding Raif and Selestra yet?" Leila asked, hope filling her eyes.

The children and Raif and Selestra seemed to be the only thing we spoke about lately.

My smile faded as I shook my head. "No, not yet. But we're still looking."

Leila let out a deep breath as she turned her attention out the window, watching the Las Vegas scenery pass by. "I have a feeling that they won't be found unless they want to be. I'm just glad Raven put a cloaking spell over the kids in New York. At least they can't find them there."

I nodded. "Yes. At least that."

We rode in silence the rest of the way, and soon, we pulled into the hospital parking lot.

"Well, we're here," I said, turning off the engine. "Why don't you go visit while I speak with Drake?"

Leila nodded, smiling, already looking more like herself at the prospect of visiting her friends again. "I'll hunt you down when I'm ready to go."

I chuckled as I placed my hand on the small of her back, guiding her toward the hospital. "Unless I hunt you down first," I teased, arching my eyebrow.

She chuckled. "Sounds good."

"There she is!" Rosa said, pulling Leila in for a hug as soon as we walked into the hospital.

I gave her a small wave and walked away, not wanting to interfere with her time with her friend. It would probably do her some good to visit with Rosa and her friends for a bit. Or at lease I hoped so.

I walked down the hallway toward Drake's office. But when I knocked, he wasn't in, so I headed toward the doctor's lounge to see if maybe he was there. But he was nowhere to be found. So, I walked out back to take in the morning sunshine. After so long of being deprived of it, now I took every opportunity I could to enjoy it.

Outside, the bright morning sunshine felt wonderful against my skin, and the breeze felt great. But all I could think about was Leila and our marriage and getting things back to how it used to be.

"Well, well, well."

My head snapped up, and Selestra was walking toward me but stopped a short distance away. "What the fuck are you doing here?" I stormed toward her. "You took my children, and now you just appear out of nowhere like I just saw you yesterday?" I quickly closed the distance between us, but she jumped out of reach when I lunged toward her, halfway up the building.

"Lance, hear me out!" she yelled, standing on a ledge three stories up.

"Why the hell should I listen to you?" I growled. "You took my children!"

"No, I didn't!" she yelled. "Please believe me!" But I reached up and squeezed the air, grabbing her by the throat as she gasped but made no effort to escape.

"You're going to pay for what you did!"

"I'm trying... to tell you... that I didn't... have anything... to do with it!" She gasped.

I threw her abruptly down onto the ground from the third story. "What the fuck are you talking about?"

"It was Raif!" she gasped. "I had nothing to do with kidnapping your children!"

"That's bullshit, and you know it!" I yelled, storming toward her, ready to take her apart. I gripped her by the throat with my cold hands and lifted her off her feet, enjoying the feel of choking the life out of her a bit too much. "Selestra, it would only take a flick of my wrist to rip your head off!"

"Lance, no!" she chocked, her feet dangling in the air. "We need to talk!"

I stared into her eyes as I held her in mid-air with one hand and then dropped her hard on the ground. "We have nothing to talk about."

"Lance, please—"

"What the hell could you have to say to me that would make a difference?" I yelled.

"I want you to go away with me," she said, her eyes pleading. "We were good together once, and we could be again—"

I walked purposefully toward her, my eyes flaring as I approached. "If you think for one moment that I could ever be with you again, you're sadly mistaken."

"Lance, I love you—"

I scoffed. "You don't know the meaning of the word," I growled, gritting my teeth as I stared into her eyes. "And if you think that I'd ever leave Leila, then you're sadly mistaken."

"But I love you, Lance—"

"Well, I hate you." I clenched my fists as I looked straight into her eyes. "And if I ever see you again, I'll rip your heart out. So, I suggest you go as far away from me as possible and leave my family alone. Because next time, I won't think twice about killing you and Raif." I laughed without humor. "Tell Raif when you see him that he's a dead man. And there is nowhere on this earth that he can hide."

She scoffed as a smile lit her lips. "Well, we'll just have to see about that."

Then in a flash, she was gone, and, against my better judgment, I let her go... this time.

The Story Concludes in:
Loved by a Vampire
(Las Vegas Vampires, #6)

PLEASE CONSIDER
LEAVING A REVIEW

ABOUT THE AUTHOR

Sophie Slade is the author of steamy Dark Romance featuring hot, powerful Alpha men and women strong enough to bring them to their knees. She has an amazing husband and three wonderful sons who collectively are the rock of her life. When Sophie's not writing, she loves horseback riding, traveling, swimming, and sitting by the pool, dreaming about killing off... er... shipping her latest characters. An American through and through and a former teacher, Sophie lives in Florida, dreaming of the day when she can write from exotic locales from around the world.

You can contact Sophie at the following venues:

E-mail: contact@sophiesladebooks.com

Facebook: Sophie Slade-Author

Twitter: https://twitter.com/SophieSladeBook

Facebook: Sophie Slade's Author Funhouse

MORE FROM SOPHIE SLADE

Las Vegas Vampires Series

Tempted by a Vampire

Seduced by a Vampire

Choice of a Vampire

Broken by a Vampire

Made by a Vampire

Loved by a Vampire

Mafia Ties Series

Chosen by Blood

Tainted Blood

Blood & Honor

Blood Birthright

Blood Bond

Blood & Lies

If Tomorrow Never Comes Duology

If Tomorrow Never Comes, Part 1

If Tomorrow Never Comes, Part 2

www.ingramcontent.com/pod-product-compliance
Lightning Source LLC
Chambersburg PA
CBHW071943120726
48001CB00005B/2013